Karmic Threads

Karmic Threads

Neelam Saxena Chandra

PRABHAT PAPERBACKS

Published by
PRABHAT PAPERBACKS
An imprint of Prabhat Prakashan Pvt. Ltd.
4/19 Asaf Ali Road,
New Delhi-110002 (INDIA)
e-mail: prabhatbooks@gmail.com

ISBN 978-93-5521-000-5
KARMIC THREADS
novel by Smt. Neelam Saxena Chandra

Edition
First, 2022

Price
₹ 350.00 (Rupees Three Hundred Fifty only)

Printed at
R-Tech Offset Printers, Delhi

Dedicated to
all those who are abused, or in pain,
but are able to carve their path with
the thousand splendid suns in their souls!

A Word of Gratitude

As a writer, my mind is always processing ideas of writing novels/stories/poems on themes that touch my heart and soul. Social themes have always stirred my mind and I have written several novels/stories about them. However, being optimistic, and having found my own path despite difficulties, I have always let my protagonists search their inner light house, which is a treasure of strength.

'Karmic Threads' deals with a grim issue. The novel also has several layers to it—the love, the treachery and betrayal, the quest and the karma (which always plays a strong role in anybody's life).

I am grateful to Raksha Hegde for being the first editor of the book. It's a pleasure to state that she has edited most of my English books. I am also thankful to Dr. Maitreyee Joshi and Meera Bhansali for going through the book and offering me useful suggestions.

I am thankful to my mother, Shashi Saxena, who is a pillar of strength and has always been there when I needed her. My daughter, Simran Chandra, has always been a companion in my journey, advising me how to better myself and giving some small tips to enhance my work; I am grateful to her.

My note would be incomplete if I don't thank my readers who have always been with me in this journey by reading my books and making them best-sellers! Thanks dear friends!

—Neelam Saxena Chandra

Contents

1

The Homeless Wanderer

Monika sat on a bench at the Trocadero, gazing at the Eiffel Tower. It was draped with electric blue lights that day, unlike the other days when the lights were yellow. Everything had changed in a matter of a split second for her. Even the lights!

The sparkle and glitter of the tower was indeed fascinating. Had it been some other day, she would have loved to watch it. It looked as if a lady had worn a twinkling light and was dancing in glory. However, that night, she found herself alone in a city of love and lights with its majestic Eiffel Tower, standing forlorn and lonely. Was the tower dancing at her despair and despondency? Was it playing a tune of bleakness and bareness?

She heard someone say, "The lights of the Eiffel Tower are turned blue on festive occasions or any other special occasion."

She wondered what it was that day that the day had pronounced upon her a sentence of misery and drabness! Was there any chance of lights in her life again? How could there be? She had come all the way from Patiala to Paris with the promise of a beautiful life and a peaceful future. Don't marriages mean this? She had been married with pomp and splendour in the traditional Indian style and she had come to Paris with the dream of a wonderful life. Alas, everything lay shattered! The truth was that she had been left alone in the world to face the reality with a few coins in hand.

People flocked at the Trocadero to catch a glimpse of the Eiffel Tower. A majority of them were tourists. She could see young lovers moving around arm in arm. A few of them could be seen kissing each other, as if kissing in front of the Eiffel Tower would make their love eternal. Tanishk had also kissed her a day after her arrival in Paris and said, "Darling, our love is so sublime, so pure. In this city of love, kissing you is like taking another vow of everlasting love. I am yours forever and forever and forever..."

He had made her feel like a divine being in those seven days. How farcical were those days and how preposterous his love! Only if she had known!

Her glance shifted to a stage which had been set up in a corner. A group of young guitarists and singers were up on the stage, for a show. Life seemed to have suddenly sprung up at Trocadero. Young and old, boys and girls – all joined the performers – some singing and some dancing. Monika watched them indulge in fun and frolic with envy. It seemed as if she was the only person who was sad. Everyone had smiles on their lips. They either had nothing to brood or worry about or they had left all their agonies at home. She couldn't do that either. After all, she had no home!

The dancing and singing went on for long and it was long past midnight when the group left. The crowd started thinning out. Finally, there were only a couple or two left. Had it been India, she would have been afraid of the dark. People said that Paris was a safe city. Anyway, she neither had any place to go nor did she have anything which she could lose now. After all, she had lost everything – her money, her jewellery and even her virginity! What more did she have to lose? The thought suddenly made her fearless. She remained seated and on finding that no one was around, she gave way to her tears. What had begun as a sob, soon turned into a wail. She had not shed a single tear since the time she had realised that

Tanishk was a crook. She had not even wept when *chacha* had expressed his helplessness in providing her solace. Now the tears had to flow and they poured like a deluge. One of the couples came near her on hearing her wail. They wondered if they could take the liberty of speaking to her! Presuming what they considered best, they silently walked away. Stories were rife all over Europe of Asians extracting money by feigning poverty and narrating stories of how they were ditched by someone and brought to Europe. May be, they thought of her too as someone who wanted to extort money.

It was the month of November and it was getting cold. However, she was so tired that she dozed off unknowingly. Tears had given her some peace of mind.

Two hours later, she was suddenly woken up due to the extreme cold. She began to shiver and her hands and feet became numb. Besides the low temperature, a cold breeze sent a chill down her spine. Now there was absolutely no one at Trocadero. She wondered where she could go to save herself from the biting cold. Suddenly she remembered the Metro station where she decided to take shelter.

The Metro station at Trocadero still buzzed with life though it was midnight. Sitting on the steps, she wondered if the people around were tourists who were enjoying the night life at Paris or if they were the locals who were going for work. She saw a female beggar sitting in the corridor with a Pomeranian dog. There was another woman who too was begging, but she had no dog. She had often seen beggars with dogs in Paris and wondered why they kept dogs with them. While sitting on the steps, an eureka moment came to her. She noticed the passers-by giving some cents to the beggar with the dog! Did the Europeans love the animals more than human beings, she wondered!

The chain of her thoughts was broken with a loud noise of 'tunnn'. She looked in the direction from which the sound came. She was shocked! Someone had thrown a cent at her, thinking her to be a beggar too! While she was still to recover from her jolt, another man threw two cents. Soon a group of youngsters passed and they gave her one Euro! What was happening, she wondered! Did she look like a beggar?

She rushed to the washroom. After relieving herself, she went and stood in front of the mirror. Her gaze fell on her own face. It was swollen due to cold and had become red at quite a few spots. Her hair was ruffled and in a mess. She looked quite underdressed in the cold of the season. Her eyes were wet. Those people who had thrown coins at her were not really wrong in mistaking her for a beggar! She looked at the mirror again and cackled loudly, initially in spurts and then at a high pitch. She began to laugh at her pathetic condition. She chuckled at her fate, chortling at her destiny.

Someone entered the washroom and seeing her cackling unashamedly, gave her a scornful look and left. She stopped for a minute, but laughed louder than what she was doing earlier. What could she lose now? Even if she was handed over to police, it would be better. They would at least deport her back to India! But what would she do there subsequently?

What indeed would she do if she returned back to her own country? *Chacha* had already made his anger known. The society would also laugh at her. And who else did she have to go to and hide her head under his patronage? Literally no one! The thought made her numb and she stopped laughing. For a moment, she watched her face again in the mirror. She washed it with water and liquid soap which was available there. She combed her hair. She looked a little better.

She went into the corridor again. A bench was empty. She lay down and wondered again at the incidents in her life of the recent past. Gurpreet's face flashed in her mind for a second and it brought a smile. However, the cold wind which had begun to blow hard made her numb again. She began to shiver. A passer-by took pity on her and placed a coat on her. She did not have the energy to even thank him.

The little warmth which she received from the coat took her in a world of sleep once again. The energy in her was fading and finally, she dozed off.

Monika kept getting disturbed dreams in her sleep. She was in the middle of a sea, with crocodiles attacking her from all sides. In order to save herself, she kept swimming without comprehending where she was going. However, soon the crocodiles were replaced by killer whales and sharks who tried to pounce on her to swallow her up. She kept dodging them for long. Finally, her energy failed her. A big killer whale was just about to attack it, when a friendly hand came and saved her. She looked up at the hand which had saved her. And she saw the face of Resham!

Monika got up, perturbed. By that time, there was a little sunlight visible. The rush at the station had increased. She got up hurriedly, afraid that someone may report her to the police. She purchased a burger from a shop. While she was gulping it hungrily, she recollected her dream. And then, it struck her!

□

2

Roopam and Monika

Certain things are bizarre. Just before Monika's marriage to Tanishk, her closest friend Resham had given her the contact details of her sister Roopam and said, "I don't know if I will get to meet you alone after this. This is Roopam's phone number. Yes, she is also in Paris, the place you are going. In case of any problems, contact her. And don't worry; she is a changed girl now." Monika had kept the contact details with her while travelling to Paris.

Since the time Monika had come to Paris, Tanishk had kept her so occupied that she had no time to think of meeting anyone. She did suggest to him once, "Tanishk, my friend's sister lives here and I think I should meet her."

He had replied, "Darling, we are in our honeymoon period at present. Let us enjoy. Once we shift into our apartment, we will obviously have a lot of time. I will take you there, after that."

She had smiled. How loving Tanishk was, she had thought that time!

Earlier itself Monika had been wary of meeting Roopam and had conveyed her request to Tanishk, only because Resham had asked her.

Monika and Resham were the best of pals, despite their differences in personalities. May be, opposites attract. Resham was not only very good at studies, but also had a melodious voice and excelled in acting. Monika was just average in everything and had no particular passion or hobbies. Monika was a quiet girl, rarely speaking to anyone, while Resham was an extrovert.

Though the two of them had never spoken to each other till they reached middle school, there certainly was an unknown attraction between the two. They would smile on seeing each other, but never entered each other's territory. Until, one day, Monika saw that Resham being scolded by their class teacher for not paying her fees.

Monika really liked Resham and she did not like the manner in which she was being scolded. She found out from her classmates that Resham's father was not able to afford her fees and was, in fact, thinking of withdrawing both his daughters from school. Monika wondered at the irony of life. She used to get an amount almost equal to their fees, as her pocket money, though she hardly used it. When her class teacher moved to their staff room after the class, she followed behind her. The class teacher asked, "Why are you here? Shouldn't you be reporting for your next class?"

She replied, "I wish to pay Resham's fees."

The teacher asked, "Why? She is not even your friend! Anyway, even if you wanted to give, you could have given in the class itself!"

Monika stated, "But Resham would have come to know and felt hurt. I don't wish to tell her that I have paid. Whenever she is not able to pay, do tell me. I will pay."

The teacher looked at her in astonishment and remarked, "May there be many more students like you."

Nevertheless, the teacher did praise Monika in the staff-room when all other teachers were present. As was to be expected, the information reached Resham's ears. She found it so unbelievable that she went and questioned Monika with moist eyes, "Monika, you don't even know me. Why did you help me? That too without any strings attached to it? Studying in school is not in the destiny of poor students like me."

Monika replied, "Because, I like you; because, I admire you; because, I didn't wish to missing from class. And as such, it is not even my money; it has been endowed to my father by God. I would have wasted it on pizzas and ice-creams. I am happy that it was put to good use."

From that moment onwards they became the best of friends. Resham's father's condition improved soon after and money no longer posed an issue. However, the fact that Monika had helped her during those bad times became a binding factor. They ate their tiffin together; they played together and they even studied together. Monika loved the food made by Resham's mother and they often exchanged their tiffin.

Their friendship remained intact even after they entered their respective colleges. She had chosen Arts with English Literature, not because she liked it, but because she had to do something after all. Her command over the language had made her mother suggest literature to her. Resham was inclined to become a teacher and took science as her subject, slowly steering her way towards her target.

During the problems which confronted Monika immediately after her admission to college, it was Resham who was with her at every difficult situation – helping her, advising her and supporting her through thick and thin.

Monika had always been afraid of Roopam, who was Resham's sister. Roopam was two years older than them. She was extremely beautiful to look at – blue coloured eyes, long straight hair and shapely body. She had also taken admission in literature at the same college and she loved it. She even helped Monika with her books and notes, till an incident occurred which changed her attitude towards Monika, turning her into an enemy.

Gurpreet was Roopam's best friend. They were childhood buddies, always sticking to each other. Monika often met him at Resham's house. However, she always respected him as her senior. He also happened to be there with her when the news of his parents' death reached her. But she took him only as Roopam's friend and nothing more.

One day, when she reached Resham's house, the latter was not there. Instead Roopam was present and she fumed with anger on seeing her, "You bitch, how could you snatch my boyfriend?"

She replied, "I don't know what you are saying, Roopam."

Roopam shrieked, "Don't act innocent and naïve at least in front of me since I know you well by now. You are a wolf in sheep's disguise. Under the garb of vulnerability and helplessness, you have deceived me."

Monika pleaded, "Roopam, at least tell me what has happened? I am absolutely clueless!"

Roopam shouted again, "Get out of my house and I do not wish to see you ever again at my place. You bought Resham by depositing her fees, you acquired my boyfriend with your money and wealth, but I am not saleable. Before I resort to violence, please leave."

When Monika reached home, a knock sounded on her door. Resham, having learnt of her sister's behavior, had come to apologise. She explained, "Roopam has always been short tempered, as you must have discovered by now, but something happened recently which has upset her. Please forgive her."

Monika asked, "But, I really do not understand what have I done to hurt her?"

Resham replied, "I think I will have to tell you the entire story. As you know, Gurpreet and Roopam had been the best of pals since early childhood. Everyone expected them to get married some fine day. Roopam kept waiting for him to propose to her, but when he didn't, she went and proposed to him this Valentine's Day. However, when he told her that it was not her whom he loved but someone else, she was shocked. And when he blurted out the name of the girl he admired, she was left speechless. She has not been able to accept the fact that Gurpreet loves someone else, but I am sure that she eventually will."

Monika asked, "Who is it whom Gurpreet loves?"

Resham replied, "I explained to Roopam that you don't know that Gurpreet loves you, but she is so upset that she does not believe me."

Monika was shocked and asked, "What? But I have hardly spoken to him, except at your house. And that too out of courtesy, since he was Roopam's friend. And yes, he also helped me in that accident, but you were there during the incident all the time, weren't you? I swear before God, Resham, I do not love him and have never met him after the incident without you. This comes to me as a rude jolt."

Resham agreed, "Don't I know that? I am sure that Roopam will realise it one day."

Monika stopped going to Resham's house after that. Of course, her bond with Resham continued as before but they met outside.

Having known that Gurpreet loved her, Monika avoided him as far as possible.

It was only after Roopam's marriage was fixed with Shekhar that she could relax. She remained hesitant to go to her place during Roopam's marriage, despite her insistence. One fine day, Roopam surprised her with a visit to her house. Handing her the marriage invitation, she said, "Monika, I am extremely sorry that I misunderstood you. It was I who loved Gurpreet; not him. Neither had he ever indicated that he loved me. I assumed that he did. I came in the way of his even declaring his love for you. It was only after I met Shekhar that I realised the situation. I will be very happy if you join me in my happiness and excuse me for my foolishness."

Monika replied, "Roopam, indeed I have no feelings for Gurpreet and neither did I have any before or now. Nor do I think I will ever fall in love with him."

Forgiving and magnanimous that she was, she joined in the celebrations. When she saw Roopam gleaming with delight, she was happy. Resham said, "Thanks for coming, Monika. Truth always prevails. Didn't I tell you that you had nothing to worry?"

Shekhar was in the Foreign Service and he kept getting posted to various countries. Roopam kept travelling and she hardly came to India after her marriage. When Resham had given Roopam's address to Monika, Monika's hesitation in meeting Roopam was obvious. It was despite the fact that Roopam had herself initiated a discussion between Gurpreet and Monika and told her, "This silly friend of mine has been in love with you since long. Why don't both of you become friends so that you can find out for yourself what sort of feelings you have for each other?"

However, despite the conflicts in the past, a flicker of light glowed in Monika's eyes. Possibly Roopam had excused her by now and wanted to help her. There was no harm in trying; after all, she had no other hope. May be...may be not.

□

3

Uncoiling

Monika checked her purse. She didn't have much money on her. Just two Euros and a few cents! She surely could not have sustained on that. She took out a cent and gave a call at Roopam's number after a lot of deliberation. On the fifth call, she picked her phone.

Monika muttered, "Roopam...I...I am...." she was at a complete loss of words. Was it alright for her to tell her about her despair? What would she think? She was about to disconnect the call.

However, Roopam stated in joy, "Hey Monika, when are you coming home? I had been expecting your call since so long! So happy to finally hear from you! How is Tanishk?"

The association to a known person was such an emotional moment for Monika that the grief which she had stored safely inside her heart, broke lose in the form of tears. She hesitatingly said, "Roopam...Roopam...Tanishk has ditched me and I am all alone..."

Before she could complete her sentence, Roopam asked, "Where are you Monika? Come to my house immediately...or wait, I think you must not be familiar with Paris. Let me come to pick you."

Monika gave Roopam her location and she was there within half an hour along with Shekhar. Embracing her,

Roopam questioned, "Why did you not call me before? Don't you trust me?"

Shekhar interfered and said, "You can surely question your friend later. Let us reach home first."

For Monika, having the comfort of a home was itself too heartening. Roopam quickly made some *alu paranthas* for her, which she gobbled as if she had never eaten before.

Roopam gave her comfortable clothes to wear and asked her to take a nap. As soon as Monika saw a clean bed, she was exuberant. She touched the bed sheet as if to ensure that she had indeed found a home. The night before, she was so sure that there was no life left for her. However, a new zest filled her bones as she lay down. And when she slept, she slept so soundly as if she had never slept before. She woke up after complete twenty-four hours.

It was a working day for Roopam and she had left for the school where she worked. However, Shekhar had taken a day off and was home. When Monika came out, he went into the kitchen to get something for her to eat. She found it a bit uncomfortable and wanted to help him out. He smiled and said, "Monika, I assure you that I cook well and do let me have the privilege of hosting a beautiful lady such as you."

Shekhar made *puri bhaji* for both of them and she was not really sure if the food was indeed really tasty or if it was her hunger which was making it appear so delicious. After they had finished eating, Shekhar said, "Consider me as your good friend or a brother or whatever you wish, but I will be happy if you reveal what actually transpired between Tanishk and you."

Monika was really happy that she had got some support during this worst phase of her life. Moreover, she knew that soon she would become a persona non grata in France and without Roopam and Shekhar's support, she could hardly do anything. However, she was not sure if she should narrate her story to him alone or in Roopam's presence. She hesitated, "Shekhar, won't it be better if I inform you about everything in

Roopam's presence lest…"

He laughed and cutting her short, said, "There is no gap or scope of misunderstanding between Roopam and me. We are one and the same. I am sure that your tale has something serious, and the sooner the fellow is apprehended, the better it will be. The scope of criminals escaping the city increases as more and more time passes."

She replied, "Shekhar, do you think Tanishk would be in France even now? He must have fled the country already. I did not know that I was dealing with a hard-core criminal."

He asked, "When did you see him last?"

She answered, "Today is the third day."

He remarked, "Oh! Shit!" and then hitting his fist on the table, asked, "Why didn't you approach us as soon as the incident occurred? You had Roopam's number, didn't you?"

She remained quiet. He asked, "I know the incident which must have made you hesitant. Was it because of that incident related to Gurpreet?"

She looked at him doubtfully. So, he knew about the incident! Roopam must have told him herself. Unsure of everything, she remained quiet.

He added, "Monika, you women can be so funny! First of all, that incident took place long back. Secondly, Roopam is already married to me. In fact, I am so thankful to the circumstances which made Gurpreet choose you over Roopam; else I would not have got to know such a wonderful companion as Roopam. I am blessed to have her as my wife!"

Monika said, "Gurpreet is a past for Roopam as well as me. But…"

Seeing her remain quiet again, he said, "Monika, on behalf of Roopam, I assure you that she does not have either hurt or guilt in her heart now. I also apologise on her behalf for her actions that time. Right now, you are her sister's friend and nothing else. And a sister's friend is like a sister only. We are happy to host you till the time you require us. However, we can assist you only if you tell us whatever happened."

She stayed silent still. He said, "Alright, let me ask you a few questions. Though I know that you were rightfully married to Tanishk, was it Gurpreet who stayed in your heart and Tanishk got angry?"

She answered, "No, Shekhar! Gurpreet understood my circumstances. If I had my own parents, I might have fought with them to get me married to Gurpreet. I could not stand up against my *chacha* and *chachi* and I accepted whatever they decided for me. Gurpreet understood this well and we parted on a happy note to meet in next life. I did inform them about my wish to marry Gurpreet, but they were quite annoyed to know it since he was not a Hindu, but a Sikh. My *chacha* was afraid that society would condemn him for getting me married to a person of my choice and that too of another religion. Gurpreet reconciled to the fact and even came to wish me for my marriage. When I decided to get married to Tanishk, both Gurpreet and I had resigned to our fate. Hence, there is no question of Tanishk having any doubts against him. I had dedicated my life to him as a humble wife."

Shekhar asked again, "You look like a much-matured girl. Was Tanishk unhappy with dowry or something? I know that dowry is a useless custom in our country and I did not take a single penny as dowry, but then men do that quite a few times. Did your *chacha* give you marriage gifts? Was he satisfied with it?"

She replied, "Yeah, my *chacha* fulfilled all his duties. Besides the vagaries of the marriage, he presented me a draft for a crore of rupees. Although that is much less than the value of my father's enterprise, but then as far as Tanishk is concerned, it was a hefty amount by any standards."

Both of them became silent after that. Shekhar wondered what other issues could be there in a marriage so as to break it in seven days! His mind wandered to many places. Was the guy a gay? Was there any other incompatibility issue? Or was there any adjustment issue? Some issues related to in-laws? Or was the guy already in love with some other girl and had married her for namesake to satisfy the urge of his parents who wished for an Indian bride? He recollected a similar incident which had taken place with one of his friend's daughter. He was almost sure that it was the reason. How someone could marry and then ditch a girl as beautiful and intelligent as Monika, he wondered.

Meanwhile, Monika was also lost in her own world of recollections. Every picture flickered though her mind, frame by frame. The sorrows as well as the happiness of the moments became as fresh as the dew drops that appear in the morning. She could still feel the grief which had seized her from all sides, making her a prisoner of fate. She felt that the feeling of her loneliness and pain was again gripping her and encaging her. She also felt the joy of having met Gurpreet and the love which he had showered on her in the arid desert of agony and ache.

Finally, she decided to open up, for she had no other option. She had to trust someone. Why not Shekhar?

She began narrating him her story, word by word.

□

4

Crooked Kins

Eight years ago, the Bajaj household buzzed with laughter and happiness emanating from every corner of the house. Mr. and Mrs. Bajaj had two children, Monika and Mayank, and always felt that they were blessed at having such adorable offspring. None of their kids was extraordinary, but they had beautiful hearts, which was how they had groomed their children.

Mr. Bajaj's business bloomed since his daughter was born and he felt that he owed everything to her. He would lovingly tell everyone, "Monika is my Laxmi, my entire wealth. Her birth brought us prosperity and she will take over the reins of my business one day."

One of the relatives asked, "What about Mayank? Normally, the business is endowed to the sons, isn't it?"

He replied, "I don't know what is normal. What I know is that we were leading such painful lives and struggling to make two ends meet when Monika was born. We stayed in a one-room tenement. There would be days when we had to skip one meal. I received the first big order along with the news that my wife is on family way and the first international order when Monika was born. From then, there has been no looking back and my business has multiplied many times. If I own this big *kothi* today along with a name in the international leather industry, it is entirely due to Monika. In fact, the business does not belong to me; it belongs to her. I am just a custodian. The moment she is of age and when she can handle it, I will pass it on to her and peacefully retire along with my wife."

The relative questioned, "What about Mayank? What will he get?"

Mr. Bajaj answered, "I am getting him well educated, isn't it enough? I am sure that he will establish a big business empire just like me some day."

However, their richness became a sore point with almost all their relatives. They were jealous on one end and talked ill about them. On the other end, they also looked at them for monetary support.

Mr. Bajaj's younger sister, Nehali Agrawal, had come to their house once and was annoyed that her brother did not have time to spend with her, though Mrs. Bajaj would take her out every day to visit some place or the other. One day, she wanted him to accompany her, despite his informing her that he had a very important meeting. She angrily began packing her things and said, "This house has no respect for me and I am leaving."

The issue went to a level where Mr. Bajaj had to finally leave the meeting and spend time with her. That he lost a big order was of no importance to her. That he lost his reputation in the market did not matter to her at all. For her, what was important was that her wish had been fulfilled. The cost did not matter.

Though Mrs. Bajaj purchased good and expensive clothes for Nehali and her entire family, but when it was time for her to return, she was again grumbling.

"What makes you unhappy, dear sister?" asked Mr. Bajaj.

"You have not given me any gold. How will I show my face to my in-laws?" she asked, "They will laugh at me and taunt me that your rich brother has nothing to give you."

By this time, Mr. Bajaj was really annoyed. He replied, "I can't give gold every time you come to my house. I treat all my siblings as equal and I have two elder sisters, one younger brother and one younger sister. Whatever I give, I shall distribute equally between all. How you convince your in-laws is your headache. Of course, I shall always be there whenever there is a genuine need, but surely not like this."

She replied, "You have insulted me, brother. Your money has gone into your head. I know who instigates you to behave like this with me. It is your dear wife, who wants everything for herself. One day, you will realise this."

Mrs. Bajaj looked at him pleadingly. Mr. Bajaj replied, "Nehali, I have had enough of you. Your blackmail is not going to work on me. Don't you dare blame my wife! She has been with me in all my ups and downs. When I did not have money, she has often stayed hungry so that I could have a meal. Another word from you and I shall sever all my relations with you."

She answered, stamping her feet in anger, "You won't have any chance of breaking relations with me, since I am not going to give you the opportunity. From today, I declare that you are no longer my brother and shall never step into your house again." She went away, fuming thereafter. She did not even accept the drive in Mr. Bajaj's car to the station. She called for an auto to travel to the station.

Soon, the news of Mr. Bajaj being arrogant, headstrong and proud was spread among all relatives by Nehali. When all his siblings gathered at one of the relative's marriage, his eldest sister Sonali said, "Arun, I don't think it suits your position to sit with us. Why don't you go and sit with people of your status?"

Mr. Bajaj got up angrily from there and went away. However, it was his wife who was left behind to bear the brunt and all the snide comments. Mr. Bajaj's second sister, Snehali asked her, "Does your daughter Monika know how to cook?"

Mrs. Bajaj replied, "No, she does not at present. However, she will learn whenever required."

Nehali mocked, "Rich men's children do not cook. They

have servants. Didn't you know it, Snehali *didi*?"

All the three sisters laughed. They were soon joined by Arun's younger brother's wife, Poonam. She added, "Just look at my daughter, Shipra. She is just one year younger to Monika and knows the entire household work. When their turn for marriage comes, I am sure that Monika won't receive a good proposal, unless it is for money's sake. After all, everyone wants a daughter-in-law who is well versed in household work."

Mrs. Bajaj said pleadingly, "Monika does know a little of everything and when the time comes, she will pick up. Cooking is not such a difficult thing. My daughter has many other gifts endowed by God."

Nehali chuckled, "Can Monika make tea?"

Mrs. Bajaj replied, "Yeah, of course! She does make tea once in a while."

Snehali summoned Monika immediately. She commanded, "Monika, we wanted to have some tea and we wish to have tea made by you."

It was the *sangeet* ceremony that day and Monika was already ready for it. She was wearing an ink blue *garara* and looking very pretty indeed. She said, "I am already decked up and it is difficult to make tea in this dress. I will ask the cook to make it and get it for all of you."

Sonali said sarcastically, "So, you confirm that you cannot make tea?"

She looked at her mother. Mrs. Bajaj, being a simpleton, was carried away by the hullabaloo around her. She gestured Monika to make tea.

When Monika went to the kitchen, her *buas* and *chachi* surrounded her. Monika was not a regular in the kitchen and she knew how to make tea by measurement. She knew that for one cup of tea, she required one teaspoon sugar and one teaspoon tea powder. When she measured that way while putting the sugar and tea, all her relatives laughed. They presumably used a piece of cloth for lifting the utensil from the gas stove. When she used the tongs for the purpose, they all giggled again. Seeing them make fun of her, she turned nervous and in the anxiety, spilled the entire tea over. While everyone laughed, she went away weeping and did not even come out for the *sangeet* ceremony or the marriage.

Such incidents when the family or one of their members was targeted and mocked at became a commonplace incident.

It was entirely a different thing that when Nehali's daughter was to get married and a hefty amount was asked by the bridegroom, it was Mr. Bajaj who paid up and made all the arrangement for the marriage. However, he felt very much unconnected with his relatives.

On Monika's sixteenth birthday, Mr. Bajaj informed both his children, "I am afraid that in case something happens to me, there will be issues and all relatives will pester you for money. I have decided to nominate three-fourth of what I have for Monika and one-fourth to Mayank. In case, something happens to either of you, then the other will get everything. I am stating in my will that your mother shall be the guardian in case you are not eighteen by then."

Monika said angrily, "What is this *bauji*? Why do you have to think about death? By God's grace, you will live long and both Mayank and I will serve you when you are old. Don't you wish to see us well settled?"

Embracing her, he said, "Darling, I know that we shall always be there for each other. Who said that I am dying? A will is made just for an emergency. I am sure that I will enjoy the loving presence of my grandchildren someday."

Monika blushed for a moment, but added, "No, *bauji!* Please don't make a will. It sounds...so awful!"

□

5
Premonitions

When Mr. Bajaj went to the lawyers to make his will, he was informed that he had to write the name of another guardian for minors besides his wife to take care of the exigencies, if both of them died. He wondered whom he should nominate. Since he had married his wife by choice, Sonam's family had discarded them. The blot of a love marriage was something they could not bear. They had maintained no relations with Sonam and had never even invited her again to the house, even when her parents died.

Finally, just because he had to nominate someone, he wrote his brother's name. He knew that such a situation was not bound to arise.

When he returned home that day, he found Monika in a tense mood. Standing in the balcony of her room, she was glancing outside. When he went and tapped her on her shoulder, she shuddered. Then she stared angrily at his face with her large eyes. Laughingly, he asked her, "What happened, *beta*?"

Her eyes were moist. Embracing him, she said, "*Bauji*, why did you have to make a will? I can't think of the world without you. I am terribly upset since the time you mentioned it. I don't need anything, *bauji*. I only need you. You should not have done it *bauji*!"

His eyes were also moist. He said, "I am indeed blessed to have a daughter like you and a son like Mayank. I also know that nothing is going to happen to me, but who knows what destiny has in store for us? It is always better to be on the safe side. After all, I do know my relatives and what they can do to amass wealth. Crooked and selfish are the only two words which can describe them. They are all after money. They know of no bonds or affection; rather, these words do not even exist in their vocabulary. I have just taken care that you have a secure future, just in case something happens to me, by writing a will."

She said further, "*Bauji,* what if Mayank has objections some day? Although as per laws, both of us should get everything equally, but it has been the tradition to will things to the son..."

His father cut her short, "Firstly, you know that I don't believe in traditions. I have always carved my own way and taken my own decisions. And secondly, Mayank always knew it. So, there can be no heartburns. After all, I got everything only because of you. If Mayank was a little older, I would have willed everything to you, but he might require money for his education."

She hesitated, "But, still...."

He replied, "Though he is too young, I have already had discussions with him. Don't worry."

Their life moved smoothly. When Monika completed her twelfth, there was a question which stream she should choose. Though she had taken science till twelfth and had done pretty well in it, she disliked it. Her father wished that she should do Masters in Business Administration, since it would prove useful in the field which she was ordained to enter. For pursuing M.B.A., any degree could suffice and that made her choice all the more difficult. Her mother had seen her read a lot of novels and poems and she wanted her to take English Honours. Monika absolutely loved the idea and would soon be found lost in literature.

In short, their life kept moving slowly and steadily. Everything looked peaceful and delightful. Little did the family realise that it was the calm before a storm!

It was a rainy day and thunder accompanied the downpour. Lightning would strike, making them tremble. Monika nestled under her father's arms and said, "I am afraid, very afraid, *bauji*."

He patted her back and said, "*Beta*, every year there are rains. I have never seen you so nervous! What has happened this time?"

She stayed burrowed under his arms and said after a long time, "I don't know *bauji*! Some thoughts are springing from inside my heart!"

He convinced her, "These are unjustified fears inside our semi-conscious mind. Don't worry! I am there!"

She remained quiet. Just then there was a knock at their door. They were surprised to see their *chacha* and *chachi's* arrival in such inclement weather. It was only after they had settled down did Mr. Bajaj understand the reason of their advent.

They had come with a marriage proposal for Monika. The guy was a rich businessman named Angad Goyal who had seen Monika at a function and was mesmerised. He was related to her *chachi* and had sent the proposal though her.

When Monika heard the proposition, she ran into her room and began to weep. Her father saw her cry and cuddling her, said, "Do you think your father will ever let you get married like this? Why do you worry till I am there? I will get my little doll married to a guy she wants. But surely, not now! You are too young for marriage. First settle down in your career, take charge of my business and then only we will consider a wedding for you. Let me handle this."

When he informed his brother about his decision, the brother replied a bit crossly, "Till now I thought that you were just a bit strong headed, but now I am sure you are foolish too.

Show some wisdom and prudence. You will never get a better proposal."

Mr. Bajaj dismissed the proposition by saying, "I am being wise and hence I am not getting Monika married at this stage. Marriage is a matter of chance; maybe, she gets a proposal better than this. Who knows the future? Anyway, I am not getting her married at this age, howsoever good the proposal may be."

Angad was a competitor to Mr. Bajaj in the leather business, though he was based in Ludhiana and not Patiala. Never had he expected that his proposal would be rejected. *Chachi* further played the role of a villain and instead of explaining to him the reasons why Mr. Bajaj had rejected the proposal, she gesticulated and said, "I don't know what my brother-in-law desires. Money has gone to his head."

Angad replied, "You will see him coming to my house with apologies and regrets. Only when he comes and touches my feet and requests me for marrying his daughter will I leave him."

Mr. Bajaj received an order for a lakh pair of gloves from a leading exporter, Mr. Parmanand Gokhlani. His samples had already been accepted. However, when his manager went to deliver the final product, he was informed that the specifications had been changed and the products were no longer acceptable. When the manager pleaded that he had already manufactured them based on the acceptance, he was shunned and driven out.

Mr. Bajaj's efforts to sell the gloves elsewhere yielded no results. His efforts to meet Mr. Gokhlani were also futile. They had been friends earlier and such an attitude left him flabbergasted. However, as if this was not enough, when Mr. Bajaj went to submit another big tender for a government supply, he was denied entry. While he was sitting in his car and pondering, he saw Angad come out of the office and sit in an Aston Martin. And then he remembered! He had seen the same

Aston Martin outside Mr. Gokhlani's office. He understood the game.

However, he took a decision immediately. Whatever may happen, he will not bow down to these tactics. How could he get his dear daughter married to such a shady and unscrupulous man?

In the evening, he explained everything to his wife, who agreed with him and said, "In the worst case, we may have to lead a life of poverty, isn't it? I am ready for it. I will also explain to Monika and Mayank and I am sure they will agree."

After dinner, Mr. and Mrs. Bajaj called Mayank as well as Monika into their bedroom and Mr. Bajaj stated, "We have called you both here so that you understand the finances which the family has."

When Mrs. Bajaj began showing them the gold and diamonds which she possessed, Monika said angrily, "What is this, *Maa*? *Bauji* writes his will and you are showing me the jewellery which we have? Will you tell us kids what is going on?"

Mr. Bajaj replied, "There is no need to be so angry, *beta*! As family members we should all have the knowledge. Bad times can strike anyone and at any moment."

She stated, "I am sure, *bauji*, there is something more than this simple reason which you are stating. I want to know it."

He informed, "There is nothing *beta*, really!" Then addressing his wife, he said, "Why don't you divide the gold and other jewellery into two parts and deposit them under two lockers – one under the name of Monika and the other under Mayank?"

Mrs. Bajaj replied, "Okay, I will do it as soon as we return from the marriage."

It was the marriage of the youngest son of Mr. Bajaj's middle sister. Earlier, even Monika was supposed to go with them. However, since her half-yearly exams had got postponed, she was forced to stay back, while others went to attend the marriage.

While leaving, Mr. Bajaj embraced Monika and winked, "It is the first time we are leaving you alone. Of course, your friend Resham has thankfully agreed to stay with you and I am grateful to her. Remember, wherever we are, we shall be there looking after you. After all, there is something called telepathy!"

□

6

Catastrophe Strikes

Monika peeped into the mirror after her parents and Mayank had left. It seemed to mock at her. The weather had been very calm when her parents had left. However, within moments, everything transformed. Winds began to blow with force, till they roared. Lightning struck every now and then with a crashing sound. A tree fell down in their courtyard with a thud.

Monika quivered again. Her heart began to beat faster and faster. There was still a lot of time for Resham to arrive. However, she could not bear the storm and gave her a call to come over early.

Though Resham had promised that she would reach in fifteen minutes, Monika found it difficult to pass even a single second. Lighting thumped again. This time, it was louder than any other time. She tried to hold on to the door at the backyard. The knob of the door came into her hand. There was a high-pitched rumble of the winds and the door flung open. She yelled loudly and fell down, either due to the suddenness of the pace with which the knob came out or due to her own fear. There was a knock on the door. The sound of the pounding increased. She was so frightened that she could not garner the strength to go and see who had come. She remained still in the position she was in. Slowly she felt that she was losing consciousness. She heard her father's voice, "I am going, *beta*. Please take care and be strong. I am sure you will ultimately be victorious despite all wounds and pain." She tried to hold him. For a moment, she could. However, he kept moving away, little by little till he faded into oblivion. She lay almost lifeless. She was aware of the landline ringing again and again in the background, but little could she do anything about it.

Resham's father was not at home when she received a call from Monika asking her to come early. Her sister's friend Gurpreet was. She requested him to drop her at Monika's house.

Since it was dark and raining heavily, Gurpreet decided to wait till Resham had entered the house. However, when he saw Resham knocking at Monika's door continuously without any reaction from inside, he became worried. He parked his bike and joined Resham.

When Monika did not open the door for long, Gurpreet got his tools from the bike and opened the door. Resham rushed inside to discover that Monika had fainted. While she rushed to get some water, Gurpreet rushed towards the phone so that he could summon the doctor. Before he could lift the phone to call, it rang once again. He took the call. Someone said in a panicky voice, "Is it Mr. Bajaj's house?"

"Yeah!" he answered.

"There has been a severe accident a few minutes back. The car in which the family was travelling has been hit by a truck. I have sent for the ambulance and police, but it looks like the case is pretty serious. Can you also hurry and reach here?" He explained the location of the accident site in detail so that they would not get confused.

Gurpreet was stunned. He was not sure if Monika needed more attention or her family members. He informed Resham, who said, "Let me call my father. He will take care of uncle and aunty and visit the site, while we take Monika to the doctor."

While Resham called up her father and explained everything, Gurpreet rushed off to get a car from his friend so that Monika could be taken to the hospital comfortably. Resham's father arranged for an ambulance to hurry to the site.

Monika was admitted in the hospital. "The girl was shocked due to something," said the doctors.

Finally, when Monika regained her senses, looking towards Resham, she asked, "Where are my parents? Where is Mayank?"

Holding her hands, Resham explained, "Monika, they had gone for a marriage, remember?"

Looking into her eyes, Monika said painfully, "No, they could not reach the venue. Some catastrophe has struck them."

"How do you know?" asked Resham.

"Telepathy, Resham. I was always connected to my *bauji* through telepathy. The connection broke a few moments before. Now the link is not there, Resham. Please find out where he is. Please find out, Resham," Monika implored.

Gurpreet, who had been listening to the conversation between the two till now, said, "Resham, let us tell her the truth. Monika, the car in which your parents were travelling has met with an accident. Resham's father has gone with an ambulance to get them. Don't worry! Everything will be fine!"

Without uttering a word, she turned her head to the other side and wept. When Resham touched her head, Monika murmured, "They will not survive, Resham, and I know it. I am all alone in this world now, I am all alone." Soon she began sobbing at first, which changed into loud wails. The doctor on duty came on a round and seeing her condition, gave her a tranquilliser shot. She began throwing her hands and feet in all directions despite the tranquilliser. The doctor then injected a sleeping drug and explained, "I think she is unnecessarily tense. This was the only option."

Resham said, "Yeah, she was alone in the house for the first time and she is usually afraid of storm and thunder."

Gurpreet asked, "Doctor, is there something called premonition?"

The doctor replied, "Strictly, in medical terms, there is no term like premonition. However, a few cases are reported every now and then, specifically when the persons involved are very close. There are certain things which science has not been able to explain as yet. You must have seen a poster in many of the hospitals, 'I treat; He heals!'"

Since the doctor asked them to switch off the lights of the rooms, Gurpreet went outside, while Resham stayed over. He saw Resham's father rushing towards him. Seeing him, he explained, "It was a bad accident. Everyone in the family is dead. There was no chance of survival. The bodies have been mutilated beyond recognition. The car got crushed badly. I am wondering about the poor kid, Monika. How will she survive this ordeal?"

Resham remained with Monika throughout the night. Next morning, Gurpreet and Roopam also joined her. The toughest thing was to break the news to Monika. Resham said, "I can't do this, I just can't! How will I tell her? Her whole world will collapse!"

Gurpreet said, "She is already mentally prepared for it. We will have to tell her. Roopam, why don't you tell her?"

She also expressed her inability for the same and hence, Gurpreet took it upon himself to do so. When she got up, sitting in front of her, he said, "Monika, I know that you don't know me much; but listen to me carefully. We have to go to your house now, but only if you promise to behave well."

She stared at him blankly and then stated after a while, "I know what you are going to tell me. My family is no more, isn't it?"

Gurpreet looked at the panic-stuck eyes. He wanted to comfort her somehow, but he could not find the words. He simply hugged her and said, "Yeah, Monika; your parents and Mayank are no more. But you are not alone and shall never be alone. We are all there for you."

She kept gazing at the empty walls in the room. He asked her, "Are you okay, Monika?"

She remained still. After some time she said, “I want to have a last glimpse of their bodies.”

Holding her hand, he took her to his car. Resham sat behind with her. She did not utter a single world during the journey.

At her house, a crowd had gathered – some out of respect for the family and some out of sheer curiosity. He shoved her through the crowd and took her carefully to the place where the mortal remains were kept.

Seeing them, she hid her face in Gurpreet’s chest and hitting him hard, kept saying, “Please get them back; please get them back! I want them, I need them!”

Embracing her tightly, he said, “You are a strong girl and you have to maintain your calm. I know it is very tough for you, but then you have to. There is no choice.”

Getting out of his embrace, she shrieked, “You are like my father only, isn’t it? He knew he was going away. He knew that I would be alone. And yet, he kept telling me to be strong. I hate him and I hate this world.” She rushed into their room and locked it from inside. Everyone could hear her howls from inside.

□

7
Permanent Visitors

Soon the Bajaj household was crammed with relatives – people whose existence was never known by Monika, people whom she had never met or heard about, people who were always averse to them. Monika was at a complete loss on how to handle these people. She had her own grief to cater to and this was an additional unwanted burden. Knowing her fully well, Resham offered to stay with her till her relatives left. She was the only person with whom Monika could connect and could discuss everything; it was a great relief.

While it was being planned to take the dead bodies to the cremation ground, a jeep with a hooter entered their premises. Mr. Shukla, the Divisional Commissioner of Police, came into their house and called for Monika. When she went outside, he stated that he wished to talk to her alone.

Mr. Shukla was a friend of her father and she knew him well. She called him inside her room. Looking at Resham, he said, "I want to discuss something important and urgent with you and I would prefer that we discuss it alone."

She replied, "Resham and I are one soul in two bodies. You can discuss anything in front of her, because, even if you don't, I will be telling her."

Mr. Shukla was a bit hesitant initially, but then he said, "Alright. Monika, I am sorry that I have to discuss this with you, but you must handle it maturedly. What I have come to tell you is that your father was a bit apprehensive of his life right from the beginning of this month. Though he did not tell me anything specific that time, but I am sure there was something which was always bothering his mind, because he did ask me how one could get police protection. Did you also notice any such changes in him, or is it a figment of my imagination?"

She stated, "To tell the truth, I too had been very concerned. He made a will and then he showed me the jewellery at home. Both his actions raised doubts and I did ask him quite a few times about it, but he never told me anything. However, he did incur a few losses in his firm as far as I could make out. Uncle, is there anything unusual about the incident?"

He replied, "Though everything sounds very normal outwardly, I have my own doubts. I have a witness who says that the truck which hit the car was parked at a place just near the site of the accident since long. My suspicions are further raised by the fact that the truck driver is missing. Do you have any suspicion?"

She looked at him wide-eyed and said, "I have no clues, uncle. May be, it is related to something in his office. I really am ignorant about this. Uncle, why did someone have to do this? Please find out, uncle and inflict the severest punishment possible."

He stated, "Of course, I shall! But I warn you also to be aware of your surroundings and everyone around you. In case of even a slight suspicion, just let me know on my mobile. Meanwhile, a postmortem will have to be conducted."

She replied, "Is there any use, uncle?"

He said, "Of course, there is. What if the persons responsible for your parents' and brother's death are after you too?"

She answered, "It is better that I die too. I don't wish to live without my family."

He explained, "God does not give you that option. You

have to survive. Moreover, just think whether your father will be happy to see you struggle and survive, or not?"

She obviously knew the answer. She remained quiet. He explained, "You carry on with your duties and let me carry on my investigation."

After he had left, Monika laid her head on Resham's lap and cried, "Why, Resham why? My father would have given anything someone wanted. Why did they have to do this to my family?"

After the postmortem, the bodies were straightaway taken to the crematorium and set on fire. What remained were smoke and ash. Smoke entered Monika's life too and everything became hazy after that. With their bodies, ash had mingled the ash of her dreams too.

One day, while she and Resham were going outside to leave Resham's mother, she heard one of her relatives say, "God knows when the lawyers will be coming to read out the will. Hope we all get something."

Another female voice said, "He was a brother to me only for namesake. I hardly got anything. That explains the condition in which he was killed. God delivers justice almost immediately."

It was then that she realised that things in her life were not bound to be simple any longer. Complications had just begun and they would only keep increasing.

The next day, the lawyers did their duty. After collecting all the relatives, they read out Mr. Bajaj's will in front of them. Things were quite clear in the will. Not a penny was given to anyone else. Everything went to Monika.

Everyone began leaving the house, one by one. There were no discussions on how Monika would be taken care of. They fretted and fumed that nothing was given by Mr. Bajaj to them.

However, there was one person who stayed over. He kept saying again and again, "Though I was never close to my brother, for he never thought me worthy enough, I consider it my duty to look after my niece, Monika. She has been endowed with all the possible wealth, but who will look after her? Who will take care of her little needs?"

Everyone was impressed. Even Monika and Resham! Resham said, "He seems to be a really nice person! Wonder why you never mentioned him?"

That evening, Poonam asked her husband, "Since when have you become so caring for your niece? Have you forgotten that we also have two children to be taken care of? This brother of yours did not give us a single pie and you are planning to stay over here to look after his daughter?"

Hanging a picture of his brother and sister-in-law on the wall and lighting a few incense sticks in front of the picture frame, he said, "Poonam, have belief in your husband. Intelligence is my strength. Did you not hear the content of the will? I heard every word shrewdly."

She asked, "What do you mean?"

He replied, "As you might have noticed, I am the guardian of Monika's wealth. Of late, my brother had lost everything due to Angad, as you and I know very well. At this point of time, his fortunes had ebbed like anything. Being the guardian, I shall take over the business and get the present worth certified legally. After that, whatever I gain shall be mine. It is as simple as that!"

She stated, "Oh! You are indeed marvellous, Varun! So, we have to continue to show her our love till the wealth is certified, isn't it?"

He answered, "My dear Poonam! You are also becoming intelligent in my company. Now, begin showering all the love and affection that you have in your heart upon Monika. She should not feel the absence of her parents. I don't mind it even if it is at the cost of our own children, Shipra and Ritesh."

She asked further, "And do we get her married to Angad now?"

He replied, "There is no need. It is very risky now after this death. I suppose you did see that police officer here. The association between us and Angad could be proved. So, it is better that we keep him away."

"But, how will we convince him?" she asked.

"It is simple. We will declare that since we began staying here, we have realised that Monika is suffering from a mental condition which forbids her marriage. Rumours spread like fire. Just remember that it should be told to others with a caution that she gets fits if anything about her condition is discussed and we have managed her with utmost care and precaution. Just do one thing, tell this to my sister Nehali, and the word shall spread. We have to do everything with an eye on the ultimate result of getting everything – this palatial bungalow, the jewellery and the business. Just dream that you and I are the owners of this bungalow."

Poonam was lost in fantasies immediately. She hugged her husband and said, "Oh! You are fantabulous, Mr. Bajaj! I am so happy that I married you!"

He planted a kiss on her lips and said, "Indeed, I am lucky too, Mrs. Bajaj! You have been a true companion to me in all my goals and ambitions! I love you for everything! I could not have got a better wife!"

□

8

Coping Up

When *chachi* asked her the next day what she wished to have for breakfast, she was taken for a surprise. She replied, "Whatever everyone will have." The recollections of the past when all her relatives had made her make tea and mocked at her were alive in her mind. She had not expected even in the wildest of her dreams that *chachi* could in reality be so caring and affectionate.

Chachi hugged her and said, "*Beta*, neither can I ever replace your mother, nor am I as good a cook as her. However, I have always considered you as my daughter and would be glad if you also consider me as your well-wisher. After all, we have to stay together now. You are too young to manage things alone."

Monika did not say anything. However, she did feel good. At least, her *chacha* and *chachi* were staying with her and taking care of her, unlike her other relatives who had vanished even before the *terahvi* ceremony.

Chachi and *chacha* took over the entire task of organising the *terahvi* ceremony. In the morning, when Monika was passing through the corridor in which *chacha* stayed, she heard him sob in front of her parent's picture hanging there, "*Bhaiya*, I am so sorry that we could never come close to each other despite both of us loving each other so much. I still remember how you used to take care of my every little need as a child. You taught me my first steps, you helped me with my first table and you coached me in the games I loved. You were always there whenever I needed you. I think it was entirely my mistake that we drifted apart on growing up. I got carried away by our sisters, especially Nehali. I really did not understand that they have become so crooked. I will replace all my misdeeds with good work and you shall see it from above. Don't worry about Monika at all; after all I am there and I shall treat her just like Shipra. The guardianship which you have entrusted upon me shall be taken care of, *bhaiya*. I promise that I will do my best. Just keep blessing me, *bhaiya*; yeah, that is all I need..."

Monika was quite touched by his tears and his words. She stood behind the door with moist eyes for long.

The *terahvi* ceremony was held with quite a lot of solemnity. "My *bhaiya* and *bhabhi* deserve the best," said *chacha*. Though none of the relatives returned for the ceremony, the home was filled with her father's friends and well-wishers from all over the town. Everyone came and narrated to her at least one story of her father's good deeds. Though he was no more, she was really proud of him. He had left behind him a trail of goodness and virtues, which elated her.

A day after the ceremony, *chacha* came into her room and asked, "I know that I had only brought that proposal of Angad; however, I find that he is not a good fellow after all. I heard a lot about his fraudulent manners and tasks. *Bhaiya* also thought it imprudent to get you married at such a young age and he was extremely against your marriage with Angad. Do you think I should put an end to the offer by refusing him curtly?"

She had been extremely worried about the proposal since the time her father had passed away. *Chacha*'s suggestion made all her fears rest and she said, "*Chacha*, do whatever you think my father would have done."

He hugged her and patting her head, said, "*Beta*, rest assured, I will not do a single thing against your wishes. If I ever deviate from my path, just remind me. I am here only to look after you and only be doing things which are best for you – that too after asking you." Monika was touched by the gesture.

One day, while they were having dinner, Shipra asked her mother, "When are we going back home? I am missing my college!"

Ritesh also added, "Yeah! I am also getting continuous calls from my school. My half-yearly exams are about to begin."

Chacha remarked emphatically, "None of you are going back. We are all shifting here to be with Monika. Shipra's college and Ritesh's school will be changed. I have already spoken to the principal of Monika's college for Shipra's admission and also in a good convent school for Ritesh's admission. I will finalise the things in next three days."

Shipra said angrily, "I am not going to change my college. Leave me in a hostel if both of you want to stay here."

Ritesh supplemented, "Do you think I can change my school at this stage? I am in class tenth and it is not a joke!"

Chacha became angry and thundered, "In this issue my diktat is going to work. Whatever I have said is my command and you are bound to agree. I will hear nothing against it."

Monika was a bit pensive and felt guilty. She went to *chacha's* room later and said, "*Chacha*, I think it is not good to change Ritesh's school or Shipra's college. Even if I had been in their place, I would have resisted it. You lose everything, including the friends. Let us think of some other option."

He replied, "Monika, why do you worry so much? Everything will fall into place. And you are a sweet girl. I know that you too would have done the same."

Monika soon adjusted to the new life. It took her time before she could finally comprehend that her parents would never come back again. But she attuned herself soon enough. With *chachi* and *chacha* always there to take care of her little things, it became somewhat easier.

One evening, she got a call from Mr. Shukla to come to his

office. When she went there along with Resham, he informed, "Monika, though I am very sure that the death of your parents was not a normal death, I have not yet been able to break through the case. Over and above this, I have got transferred to Amritsar. Though I shall be requesting the next DCP to keep chasing the case, I am not sure about the outcome."

She replied, "Let it be, *chacha*. You did your best. Certain things are destined, isn't it? I have accepted everything."

That night she remembered things that her father used to say. How lovely those days were! She decided to concentrate on what her father wished her to become – a successful entrepreneur, looking after his business empire.

Till her parents were alive, she did not have much inclination for studies. However, with a change in the situation, she found herself getting more and more involved. She used to love literature, but now it became her passion. She began spending most of her time with books.

Resham, being a true friend that she was, always found time for her despite her own busy schedule. Whenever Monika felt low, she was there to raise her spirits; when Monika felt lost, she made her feel that in fact she was always victorious and when Monika apprised her of her intentions to study well, she gifted her lot of books. Resham's parents also understood the bond between the two of them and never came in the way of their friendship.

One day, when she returned from college, *chacha* called her and said, "I have got the assessment of your father's enterprise done by a Delhi-based firm whom your father always trusted. I have called them today, along with the lawyers and chartered accountants of your father. I desire that you should also join us. After all, it is your enterprise which I am running on behalf of you temporarily till you are old enough to take charge."

She replied, "*Chacha*, I am fine with whatever decision you take. I don't wish to get involved at this stage. I will surely join you when I am older."

He stated, "But it is my earnest request to you, *beta*."

She said, "Alright, *chacha*! Since you have asked me to be with you, I shall. However, I shall just listen to everything, but not comment upon anything. At seventeen, I am too young to apprehend the rules of business."

After everyone arrived in the evening, the Managing Director of the firm from Delhi, while presenting his report, stated, "We have taken into consideration all the figures and facts and the value assigned to the firm is exactly ninety lakhs." The various parameters adopted and assumptions taken were explained by him to everyone. Finally, after everyone had read the report, her father's lawyer said, "I think you have done a wonderful job, Mr. Shetty." Then addressing *chacha*, he continued, "I think you can pick up the work from here, Mr. Bajaj, since you are the legal guardian of Monika now."

□

9

Gurpreet

Monika's life kept moving smoothly. Unaware of the storms that were building and ready to strike anytime; she kept moving ahead in life slowly. She thought that the biggest tornado in her life had already passed and there could be nothing worse than that. The space which was left by her parents remained blank and she knew it could never be filled, but she had learnt to move on.

Gurpreet was a handsome guy. He always remained the focus of attention of everyone because of his looks. His height was a matter of envy to all guys. He was well-built and had a smart gait. There was freshness in his face which could not really be defined, but felt. And it was experienced by the girls wherever he went. He would always be flocked by girls trying to gain his attention. He despised the attention and would prefer to be alone, to the chagrin of the girls. While the guys would ask him, "What do you eat which we don't, to attract everyone around?" he would wonder what all the talk was about and why was he not left alone.

His desire and his nervousness were both understood by his classmate Roopam and they became the best of friends. Once, while he was being swarmed by the girls, Roopam came to his rescue as usual and said after that, "I think I have a plan. If you do what I say, no girl will ever trouble you."

He asked, "What is that? I am ready to do whatever you say. But I have these girls who try to gain attention."

She replied, "Let us both spread the rumour that we are going steady and I am your girlfriend."

He asked innocently, "But, I don't consider you as a girlfriend. I think we are simple friends."

She grinned, "Who is asking you to be a real boyfriend? I also know that. But let us fake it for the others. This is just to keep those girls away from you."

He questioned once again, "What if I like some girl some day?"

She replied, "I can also like some boy someday. Then, we will tell everyone that we had faked this relationship. Isn't it simple?"

He smiled and said, "You are a genius, Roopam!" and they did a hi-fi.

The news soon spread like wild fire. Both of them did not mind it. They were happy to be in each other's company and did things they enjoyed together. First and foremost was their love for good books. Both of them would read the same novel and then discuss and debate on every dialogue and every incident. Their world was small. The things did not change even when they entered college. They even began visiting each other at their homes and both their parents understood their friendship.

However, things took a turn when Gurpreet saw Monika, who was Roopam's sister's friend. He was completely awestruck. And, for the first time, there was a girl who did not show any interest in him! This attracted him all the more towards her. The desire to know her more kept mounting and he would purposely be at Roopam's house whenever he heard that Monika was coming.

One day, Resham asked him to leave her at Monika's house and while he waited outside, he saw that no one responded to Resham's knocks. The moment coincided with the news of Monika's father's death and he just couldn't bear to see her in distress. When he took her in his arms to comfort her, he was sure that he wanted to be with her in all the upheavals of her life.

However, when he informed Roopam about his love for Monika, she was flabbergasted. Though they had faked their affair and had both decided that it was only for the world, Roopam had become attached to him and had begun loving him. Since he valued their friendship a lot, he decided to wait for her till she accepted the fact.

That time Monika was sure that the feelings which she had for Gurpreet were surely not love. She had also said, "I can never fall in love!" However, one can never say 'never', isn't it? The more she refused, the more she was drawn towards the character who loved her without even telling her. She wondered what made him love her when he had such a lovely friend as Roopam, who was head over heels in love with him.

When she came out of her college a day after Roopam's marriage, she found him standing outside her college under the tree, right in front of the gate, looking at her. She glanced at him, but walked past him.

She was surprised to find him standing there the next day and the day after that. She could find him waiting at the same place for a whole month. One day, it was raining very hard and yet, he stood there, waiting for her. Monika went to him and asked, "What do you want?"

He answered, "You!"

She asked, "Why?"

He replied, "Because I love you! I am sure you heard about it from Resham earlier. And didn't Roopam tell you about my love?"

She stated, "I hardly know you to love you. I always respected you as Roopam's friend. Nothing more. It came as a shock to me when Roopam fought over it. And you also hardly know me. How can you love me?"

He said, "Will you agree to come and sit with me in the canteen? At least listen to me. At least give me some time to express my views."

She said, "Alright. Ten minutes."

They went and sat in the canteen. Since it was raining, there was hardly anyone around. She said, "Tell me."

Gurpreet stated, "Monika, though I was a close friend of Roopam, I never loved her. I always felt that we were more like siblings. Whenever I would see you at her house, I would get a feeling that this is a girl who is a bit different than the rest – a girl who is unaffected by the impurity and politics surrounding the world, a girl who is naïve and innocent and a girl who needs to be protected against the cruel world. I don't really know if I fell in love with you at that moment or if it was when I came to your house that day when that catastrophe took place leaving us all bewildered. My mind was set – if I ever wished to marry, it had to be you or no one else. However, before proposing to you, I decided to discuss the issue with Roopam, just because she was a good friend."

The tea which they had ordered arrived by then and he sipped a little from the cup and then continued, "When I told Roopam about my love for you, she was flabbergasted because she had always loved me. I could not have loved her the way she wanted, for her image in my mind was completely different, as you must have understood. However, being an old friend, I honoured her feelings and did not get in touch with you. She remained annoyed with me and I waited for her to reconcile. It was only when she finally got married to Shekhar happily, that I thought of asking you."

She said, "I am quite touched, Gurpreet; but I have no such feelings for you. Hope you understand!"

He expressed, "Yes, I do! However I also know that you will begin loving me one day. I believe in my love and I am ready to wait for you forever."

When she did not reply anything, raising his hand for a handshake, he asked, "Friends?"

She replied, "Yeah, friends!"

He asked, "Do you promise to meet me once in a while so that we get to know each other?"

She replied, “Alright, but I will meet you only in the presence of Resham.”

He smiled and said, “As you wish, Madam!”

She asked, “Can I take your leave now?”

He smiled again. He saw the girl of her dreams walking away. Her lengthy plait made out of her straight hair was swinging to and fro. It suited her height. He kept watching her for long as her size kept diminishing and finally became a tiny dot. Then, after paying the bill, he went home with satisfaction glowing on his face.

□

10

Doting Company

When Resham came to her house a day later, she found Monika's face glowing unusually. She was listening to a romantic number, completely submerged. Resham teased her and asked, "So Monika, what is new in your life?"

Monika grinned and said, "Nothing dear!"

Resham laughed, "I know there is! I can make out from the expression on your face! We know each other since long now to hide anything. Will you tell me or..."

She blushed and said, "Someone proposed to me!"

Lifting Monika's chin with her index finger, Resham asked, "And what did Miss Beautiful reply?"

She removed Resham's hand and said, "Nothing as yet!"

Resham asked, "Why?"

Monika kept fiddling with her long plait, but kept quiet.

Resham asked, "Because of Roopam?"

Monika questioned, "How do you know?"

Resham said, "There is something called gut feeling. In fact, Gurpreet has been in love with you since long. He remained quiet because of Roopam's fury. Though I was aware of everything, I didn't say anything because I knew that time will itself remove the clouds of darkness and show a glow. Thankfully, it happened soon. You can say that I have been an accomplice in his love story."

Displaying false anger, Monika said, "This is not done! Are you my friend or his friend?"

Resham laughed, "Of course, I am your friend first and then comes anyone else. And it is only because I knew that he is 'the' right match for you that I became a co-conspirator."

Monika stated, "I wonder though what he saw in me!"

Resham laughed, "You are really sweet, Monika! You are so gifted and talented, but you don't know yourself. One should not be over-confident, but I want you to be a bit more poised. It was sweet of Gurpreet to wait for Roopam to settle down and then propose to you. And I think you should chill, let your hair loose and enjoy the feeling of being in love."

Monika answered, "I will try. I am not so sure, though if I too am in love with him."

Resham asked, "What? You have not yet replied to him? So silly of you!"

Monika stated, "I want to be sure of myself before I commit to anyone. It won't be fair without that!"

Resham said, "Okay! Take your own sweet time! But the day you accept his proposal, you both will take me out for a treat. Agreed?"

Monika replied with a smile, "Yes, agreed! Resham, you are a person dearest to me. How can I celebrate anything without you?"

Soon it was Resham's birthday. Her parents had gone out. She called over a few friends to celebrate the day with her. She played a naughty trick. Although she had called everyone at 6 p.m., she informed both Gurpreet and Monika to come at 4 p.m. and sent them together to get cakes and ice cream.

Togetherness was something that gave them both a delight. While Gurpreet drove the Mercedes, Monika sat next to him. He asked, "When will I get my answer?"

She blushed. When he repeated the question, she said, "Remember, we both agreed to be friends?"

He grinned and said, "You girls are incorrigible."

She smiled, "Now, what does this question mean? What is my fault?"

He chuckled, "Though you also love me, you will not accept it."

By that time they had approached the confectionery shop. Monika knew by heart that Resham ate only chocolate cake and she asked the shopkeeper to pack it. She got busy with instructing him what should be written on the cake. She saw that Gurpreet had gone somewhere and wondered where he was. He soon returned with pieces of mixed fruit pastry. She asked, "What is this?"

He replied, "Don't I know that you don't like the taste of chocolate?"

She asked, "How did you find out?"

He answered, "Your friend Resham. I have made a full diary of what you like and what you don't like."

While both of them ate the pastry, she asked, "But which pastry do you like?"

He replied, "Chocolate."

She asked, "Then why are you eating mixed fruit?"

He answered, "Because you like it. And your wish is my command."

She laughed and said, "You are a moron!"

He replied, "Yeah, I am one. And it seems I am bound to remain so for long since the lady I love does not reciprocate!"

She questioned, "So once I accept, you will start eating chocolate pastry once again?"

He cackled, "Did I say that? Monika, my love is not an infatuation. It is something more than that. My love is forever. You can test me if you want. For me, there is no other girl and there shall be none. Either it has to be you or no one."

Giving him a friendly pat, she said, "Time tests everyone.

Don't worry. Come, let us go and get ice-cream, otherwise we will get late."

However, he didn't move an inch and stood where he was. When she came back to look for him, he said, "Let time test me as much as possible. I am ready for it. You won't get a person as loyal and as sincere as me."

After purchasing ice cream, they returned back. Resham's guests had started arriving by then. There was a lot of singing and dancing. Though Monika had never danced before, Gurpreet was a wonderful dancer. He excelled at Salsa. When it was his turn to dance, he invited Monika too. She said, "I have never danced before and I just can't. It is not my cup of tea."

Holding her hand, he said, "Just let yourself loose and I will make you dance. I know that you will dance amazingly."

Since everyone insisted, she joined him. His right hand was on her waist, while he held her left hand. Her right hand automatically went on his shoulders. Just as he had said, she just followed him. And slowly, she learnt the steps. One song ended and the other began. Everyone wanted to see more of their dance. They too had no wish to discontinue. They kept dancing for long, lost in each other. After the songs in the DVD got over, there was clapping by everyone and they halted. Monika coyly went and sat in a corner. She had enjoyed every moment, but was reluctant to admit it, even to herself.

After the party was over, Monika's driver had not come since he was busy with Shipra, so Gurpreet offered to drop her. He put on the same DVD on whose songs they were dancing a little while ago. The air inside the Mercedes was full of romance. They remained quiet for quite some time. Finally, Gurpreet broke the silence by asking, "Monika, are you afraid?"

When she did not reply, he questioned again, "Are you afraid of me or are you apprehensive of falling in love?"

She was still quiet. Halting the Mercedes, he said, "I want

an answer, Monika. You are free to say that you dislike me. But you can't remain quiet."

She said, "Please drive. I will talk as you drive."

Gurpreet started the Mercedes. After a little while, she said, "Gurpreet, it is not you. I have nothing against you. I won't say that I love you, but I do like you. You are a guy any girl would be pleased to fall in love with. I am in general, scared of loving anyone anymore. I adored my father, my brother Mayank and my mother. They all left me. I am frightened that if I love anyone, the person will also leave me and go away, leaving me broken-hearted. I am afraid of loving anyone."

With his left hand, he held her hand and said, "I can understand your apprehensions, dear. But you love Resham also, isn't it? And she has remained a loyal and sincere friend, isn't it?"

She nodded.

He continued, "Moreover, none of us know what destiny had inked for us. No two persons can remain together for their lifetime. That we could spend some time in a fond company gives us the energy and enthusiasm to live, isn't it? Are you not happy that your parents loved you so much? How many persons in this world get such a sublime love?"

She was speechless. After some time, she said, "You are a philosophical person! For the first time after my parents' death, I am really feeling alright. I could not really get used to staying without them. It has been really difficult. It is almost as if I am alive, but my heart is dead. I don't say that my *chacha* and *chachi* do not give me love – they do! But then, something is still missing...I miss my parents! I will try to see it in the light of your new philosophy."

By that time, they had approached Monika's house. He asked, "Will you meet me tomorrow?"

She asked, "Where?"

He replied, "Where else? Resham's house! It is the best place to meet!"

She said, "Alright, I shall try!"

He stated, "I shall wait for you at her house at 5 p.m. Do come!"

While she removed her seat belt, he held her hand once again and taking it towards his lips, planted a kiss on her wrist. He said, "Good night! Sweet dreams! See you tomorrow!"

□

11

Love Blooms

Next day, Monika spent her entire time wondering what she should wear. Her glance automatically kept going to the mirror. As evening approached, she tried one dress after another, rejecting all of them. Finally, there was a pile of clothes on her bed, worn and discarded. She looked at the heap and sat sullenly. Suddenly, she remembered a pure white *anarkali* suit with golden work and she took it out from her wardrobe.

Just then, Shipra entered her room and said, "Hey Monika! Wondering what to wear? But I am seeing that you are doing it for the first time; otherwise, you wear whatever comes in front of you! I hope you are not in love by any chance!"

Monika never really got along with Shipra, who always considered her as a competitor. Shipra always had some issues or the other with her, despite her maintaining her silence and serenity. Shipra rarely came into her room, unless she had some work. Shipra's glance fell upon the *anarkali* suit which she was holding and she jumped in joy, "This was the sort of dress I was looking for! Will you lend me for a day?"

Monika was in a dilemma. If she refused her the dress, she would raise a hue and cry. If she gave it, she would be unhappy, since she had set her mind on it. Things changed so much! Till her parents were alive, she didn't have to think twice before stating her wish. She had simply stopped wishing since long now. And whatever little she had, she could not really own it. She felt that she had become an outsider in her own house. She gave away the dress to Shipra without a fuss and sat down gloomily. Finally, when it was almost five, she wore a simple Capri and a red top with white polka dots and proceeded to Resham's house.

She was late by ten minutes and she found Gurpreet waiting eagerly for her. He had worn a suit for a change. She looked at him keenly and said to herself, 'Indeed he is a handsome chap! And caring too! I wonder why I am taking so much time to accept his proposal!'

Resham, as usual, wanted that they should spend some time alone and after offering them some coke, said, "Listen guys, I have to purchase groceries, since *beeji* and *bauji* are scheduled to arrive tomorrow. I hope you don't mind my going away for some time."

Both of them were actually happy and simply nodded. However, the moment Resham was gone, Monika felt a little uncomfortable. Guessing it, Gurpreet said, "Don't worry, Monika! I love you and I will never do anything which will hurt you or make you regret it. Let us just talk as friends. Isn't it a good occasion to know and understand each other? I think it is!"

That made her relaxed. He stated, "Monika, you not only look really beautiful, but have a beautiful heart too. Your beautiful heart was what attracted me towards you in the first place. Do you understand what I am trying to say?"

She smiled and said, "I am trying to. But I really don't know how to let go. There is something which binds me. There is something which stops me from moving ahead. I know that you are a very wonderful person and any girl would feel privileged to get your attention…and I too should…but…"

He asked her, "Is there anyone else in your life besides me?"

She replied, "No, there isn't. Neither has any male ever interested me other than my father."

He kept quiet as if trying to comprehend her thoughts. Then he said, "Tell me more about your father."

It was as if she had bottled up all her emotions and they were let loose the moment she got some sympathy from another understanding soul. She kept narrating incident after incident, including the proposal of Angad. Finally she said, "Gurpreet, I think I am still not normal. Though everything seems fine outwardly, but I miss my father, my mother and Mayank every moment. I just don't know how to live. My *chacha* and *chachi* do try their best to make me feel comfortable...but...there is something missing. I feel that he was like an umbrella over my head, protecting me from summer, winter and rains and now that umbrella is gone, gone forever."

Gurpreet, out of raw reaction of the moment, embraced her and said, "Monika, I can understand every bit of what you said. And...and whether you love me or not, I shall always be there for you. I can never take your father's place, but I will try my best to be a good friend forever and always."

Her eyes turned moist. She felt very comforting in his embrace. And then she remembered. It was the same embrace which had given her comfort when the news of her family's death had reached her. The cuddle did have a serenity which was at a plane higher than raw love. She also hugged him and looking into his eyes, uttered, "I love you, Gurpreet; I do! But I am afraid, very, very afraid, Gurpreet! Will you love me forever and forever? And...and are you sure that you will never leave me alone?"

Giving her a peck on his forehead, he said, "Never, Monika, never! How can I leave you, Monika? From this moment, I give you my heart and my soul forever and forever and forever. I can't tell you how much happiness you have gifted me by reciprocating my love!"

She rested her head in his arms again. In the embrace, she found a solace which she had never found since her father died. She remained in the state for long. Gurpreet lifted her mouth by putting his finger on her chin. They faced each other and remained locked in the state for long, gazing into each other's eyes. Automatically, she took her lips towards his and they kissed each other.

Monika suddenly got up and moved away from him. He smiled and asked, "What happened?"

She asked, "What if we are not able to get married?"

He said, "From my end, there are no problems. My parents have given me full freedom to marry a girl of my choice. But, it may be tough convincing your *chacha* and *chachi*. After all, they wanted someone like Angad for you, who happens to be a millionaire. As you know, I have just started my publishing venture. Of course, besides that, my father's business is still very good. But we are certainly not at Angad's level. I can promise you that you will never have any difficulties. You will just have to utter something and it will be there."

She said, "I will convince them. I have always lived an extravagant life and I know that it is not money which is most important in life. Love certainly is. It is affection and fondness which binds a family. Money comes and goes."

He stated, "So happy to know your views, Monika. Though we had never discussed, but I knew that you think like this. I am blessed to have you in my life."

She again came nearer to him and embracing him, said, "So am I! Never have I felt so wanted and so loved in the last few days."

He said, "To mark this day, I have got something for you, dear!" From the pocket of his trousers, he took out a little casket. Inside it was a delicate diamond ring.

Looking at it in amazement, she asked, "Did you know that I will accept your proposal today?"

He grinned, "Yes, I did. I purchased it yesterday."

Then, kneeling in front of her, he took her hand and slipped the ring on her ring finger. He asked, "Will you be my sweetheart forever and forever and forever?"

She blushed and looked down. With his finger, he lifted her chin again and asked, "I am waiting for your answer!"

She also kneeled on the floor so that she came at his level. Then she kissed him again and then said, "I hope you got your answer."

He smiled and embraced her.

Just then, there was a knock on the door. Resham had returned back. Seeing the smile on Monika's face, she asked her mischievously, "So you have finally agreed to Gurpreet's proposal?"

She ran away. Resham came inside the room and addressing them both, said, "I am so happy that the best of my pals are in love! May God grant you all the happiness in life!"

Looking at Gurpreet, she said, "My friend Monika is the most adorable character in the world, but she is highly fragile. I request you never to break her heart."

He stated, "Resham, I promise in front of you that Monika is my life now and I shall take utmost care to keep her happy and satisfied."

Resham had got *samosa* and *chaat* for them and after they had eaten, Monika said, "It is time that I should go home. Otherwise, my *chacha* and *chachi* shall worry."

Gurpreet said, "Let me have the honour of dropping you home." She smiled and both of them went away.

After they had gone, Resham prayed in front of God, "Monika deserves the best in life. After all, she has always loved. Please don't give her any more hurts, God!"

□

12
The Struggle Begins

Happiness glowed on Gurpreet and Monika's face as they drove to her house. Full of contentment at having found each other, they kept talking as if there was no end. While they approached her house, he said, "Let us take a long ride again. I haven't had enough of you. I want more of your divine company."

She smiled and gave her consent. They had so much to talk about. Even a long ride could not fulfil their hearts. After they reached her house again, he said, "Should we go in repeat mode till infinity?"

She laughed and said, "Leave it now. You talk like an engineer and I hate the left-brained persons. They are emotionless. Anyway, it is quite late and my *chacha* and *chachi* may worry. We will meet again. What makes you anxious?"

He stopped the Mercedes at a little distance from her house. Taking her lips in his, he kissed her again. She coyly said, "Let me go now. We will meet again soon."

He asked, "Promise?"

"Yeah!" she replied, "Gurpreet, when will you take me to meet your parents?"

"I think it is better that we wait at least for a year. By that time, I will settle down in my business and I will be able to give you a life which you are used to! And…and don't worry about your *chacha* and *chachi*. I will myself come and explain to them everything and ask them for your hand."

Soon, the results of her post-graduation in English were declared and she had done extremely well in the exams. *Chachi* said that day, "I am very proud of you, *beta*! Now that you have finished your studies, I think it is time we start looking for a suitable groom for you."

The thought worried her. Unsure of what she should reply, she said, "Just give me a year more. I wish to complete Bachelors in Education." She had not really given it a thought, but just because one of her classmates was planning to do it, she stated it randomly. She just wished to pass time till Gurpreet was ready to ask for her hand in marriage.

"Bachelors in Education? From where did you get this idea all of a sudden? You were never inclined to teaching? In fact, as far as I remember, you pined for a degree in Business Administration!" *chachi* exclaimed.

"That was before my father's death," she replied.

Although Monika was not at all interested in studying B.Ed., she took admissions in a college for completing the same. After all she would get a breather.

Life kept moving. Another year passed in a jiffy. Monika completed her B.Ed. Gurpreet's business also picked up. One day, he said, "I would like you to come and meet my parents."

Monika was extremely anxious, thinking of the same. With the help of Resham, she purchased a new Patiala suit. She wanted to feel good as she went to meet them. Her new dress might cover up the nervousness which she felt all the while. She put on *kajal*, eye shadow, mascara and also a little of lipstick. When Gurpreet came to receive her, he was amazed to see how pretty she looked with a little makeup. Holding her hand, he said, "You need not be so nervous, dear! I am sure that you will love my parents. They are very adorable and they have been waiting since long for me to get married. They would be happy to see that I have chosen such a beautiful girl as my bride. And they know all about you, since I have told them everything and also shown them your photograph."

His touching gesture lessened her unease. And when she actually met his parents, she wondered why she was so apprehensive. His mother had made a lot of dishes of her choice to welcome her. She said, "Welcome home, *beta*! Since so long I have desired to hand over everything to my daughter-in-law but my son was not giving me the pleasure. Finally, when he has agreed, he has come home with such a loving, caring and beautiful girl! I am so lucky!"

She spent some wonderful time with them. When she got up to leave, Gurpreet's father said, "If required, I will come and personally ask for your hand. I am sure Mr. Bajaj will approve of the proposal."

Gurpreet came to leave her back. As usual, he stopped his Mercedes at a distance little away from her house. Kissing her, he winked, "Didn't I tell you that you will win over the hearts of my parents? I am sure that your *chachi* and *chacha* will also love me. I am waiting for the day when you will come to my house dressed as a bride! You should wear a turquoise *lehenga* on our wedding – you look awesome in this colour!"

That day also she had worn a turquoise Patiala suit and she smiled. She had a sudden urge to embrace Gurpreet and kissing him back said, "Gurpreet, whenever I am very happy, something usually happens to make me sad. Will you be there to stand by me if I am in any trouble?"

He replied, "Is this a question to ask? I am your soul-mate, dear. Your wish shall be my command. You just have to tell me and it shall be done!"

She hugged him tight and looking into his eyes, asked, "Is it a promise? You will do whatever I say?"

He replied, "Yes, Monika! It is a promise!"

While their eyes were locked, they heard the sound of footsteps nearby. Monika looked around and saw her cousin Shipra rushing home. She was sure that Shipra had seen her. She trembled and said, "The girl who just passed by was

Shipra. I am sure that she has seen us. I am sure that problems await us."

He cuddled her again and said, "There cannot be any hindrances. I am ready to face your *chacha* and *chachi* and say with my head held high that we are both in love with each other and I wish to marry you. So, where is the hitch? If you wish, I will come along just now."

She replied, "No...let me see what awaits me at home."

He stated, "But, you will have to promise that you will call me in case of any difficulties. Will you?"

She replied, "Yes, of course! Who else do I have?"

He lifted her chin high and looking into her eyes, said, "Monika, please do not be afraid. We have not done anything wrong. And whatever we have planned, we are in it together. You and I are same. We are not different. Alright?"

She nodded. And then releasing herself from his grip, she got down from the Mercedes and rushed home.

Shipra had seen Monika and Gurpreet kissing each other. She went home and shouted at her mother, "What sort of a Mom you are? You always side with Monika for everything, though it is me who is your real daughter. Do you like me even a bit? You always have problems with my boyfriends, don't you? What about Monika? You don't have any issues with her, isn't it?"

Her mother asked, "What about her? Why are you always so jealous of her? After all, she is your elder sister. And remember, we are staying in a house rightfully owned by her."

She replied, "She is having a nice affair with a *sardar*! I just saw them getting cozy in the Mercedes. Now I am waiting to see what your reaction will be and what you say to her."

Her mother kept quiet at that moment, but as soon as her husband came, she informed him and added, "All our plans will go haywire if Monika gets married to someone in Patiala. She and her husband will take control of the entire business and all our efforts of so many years will be a sheer waste. I have disregarded Shipra so much just because we can finally get what we want. She is always upset with me and yet, I can't explain anything to her since you have bound me from doing it. And now this! Shit! My head is bursting. "

"Don't worry, dear! Where there is a will, there is a way. I had been looking for a proposal from outside the country for Monika since long. Only today, I had received a call from someone who is working with a big multinational in France and has come to India in search of a bride. That time I was in a meeting and had not talked much. Let me call him up. And you will not discuss anything that Shipra has told you with Monika."

"What if Shipra tells her? How do I stop her?" she asked.

"Send her to your sister's house for some time. Fake any emergency," he ordered. Soon he made a call to Tanishk and began discussing with him about the possible alliance with Monika.

□

13

The Marriage Proposal

After a long discussion with Tanishk Monga, Varun Bajaj summoned his wife and said, "The dowry demand from the groom's side is quite huge. However, the guy sounds nice. No one will ever raise a finger against my action. He is the vice president (Finance) of Deere International, which has its headquarters at Paris. Quite an achievement indeed at such a young age! He has studied from Indian Institute of Management, Ahmedabad. I am sure that all this will shut the mouths of all those loyal to my brother and also all relatives."

"How much is the dowry demand? Is it beyond our means?" Mrs. Bajaj asked.

"Of course, not! It is very much within our means. I have summed up everything and it comes to around ninety lakhs. He wants a Chevrolet Captiva for his parents, a three-bedroom flat in Chandigarh for them and a good marriage. A flat in Chandigarh should cost around fifty lakh and a Captiva should be around fifteen lakhs. Above this, the kind of marriage he is looking for should be around twenty-five lakhs. This is approximately equal to the amount which was the worth of the business when I took charge. Thus, in all, the entire proposal seems viable. No profit, no loss," Mr. Bajaj informed.

"What is the present worth of the business empire built by you?" Mrs. Bajaj asked.

"It should roughly be around twenty crore," he stated.

"Oh! And this increase is entirely an effort of your sweat! Remember your brother was running at a loss before his death. I think we should go ahead with the proposal. After all, it is peanuts as compared to what you have now."

"Yes, I have called over the guy and his family tomorrow at our house. Now, it is your duty to convince Monika."

"I can't do it alone. You will have to be there with me."

"Why are you so fearful of asking?"

"I won't know how to deal with her if she talks about the guy she loves."

"Oh! If that is your worry, it is simple enough. Shipra had informed that the guy is a Sikh, isn't it."

"Yes."

"We don't get our girls married to a Sikh. It is as simple as that. We marry in our own religion!"

"Still, I will prefer that you come with me."

Monika was listening to a song on television, when *chacha* and *chachi* entered her room. Seeing them enter, she was very apprehensive and knew that there was an imminent problem lurking over her head.

Chachi asked, "Monika, I hope that we have fulfilled the duties of guardianship well. We have tried our best but still if there are issues, we are both extremely sorry."

Monika became very sentimental. She said, "What are you saying? I had no one after my parent's death and you both took care of me even more than what you would have done for your own daughter."

Chacha said, "*Beta*, now it is the time for us to fulfil our last important responsibility, after which I will be able to tell your father when we meet in heaven that I did a good job."

She wondered where the conversation was going and stared at both of them questioningly. It was *chachi* who answered, "Monika, we have been looking for a suitable groom for you and we have shortlisted Tanishk for you. He is all that a girl may desire. You will of course see him tomorrow when he comes to meet you, but he is indeed the best. He is well placed with a good multinational and is located at Paris."

Monika hesitated. She was not sure if it was the right way to disclose about her and Gurpreet. But she did not have an option. She finally murmured, "Actually, *chacha* and *chachi*...I...I am in love. The guy is a very nice guy. He has his own business of publishing. His father is Mr. Makkar, the well-known businessman. I...I wish to marry him. He will come to talk to you whenever you wish."

"What? How can you do this, Monika? Did we dedicate our entire life and leave our own house and business to stay with you to hear this someday? People are correct when they say that someone else's children cannot be your own. Where did we go wrong, Monika?" said *chacha* with moist eyes.

She stated apologetically, "It is not that way, *chacha*! He is genuinely a nice guy. You should meet him once and you will know."

He replied, "I know the guy you are talking about. In a city like Patiala, everyone knows everybody. But didn't you think twice before thinking about him as your husband? He is not from our religion. We Khatris do not marry a turbaned Sikh!"

She said, "All that is an old-fashioned talk, isn't it *chacha*? The marriages between Khatris and Sikhs are a very common thing in the modern era."

He said loudly, "Monika, I just want to say one thing. If it had been Shipra who had come up with such a proposal, I would have slaughtered both – my daughter as well as the guy she loved. The family honour is the most important thing. Yes, call me old fashioned, but I do believe in it."

Monika remained quiet. *Chachi* said, "Monika, just think deeply about what your *chacha* is saying. Try to understand him, *beta*. After all, he has devoted his entire life to help you and bring you up properly."

Chacha sobbed, "I don't know what face I will show to my brother. He will think that I did not take care of his family, even after his death."

Seeing him sob, she was touched. She had never seen a man weeping. For a moment, she felt that she had indeed committed a crime by falling in love with Gurpreet. Getting out of her room, he said grimly, "I sincerely believe you should reconsider the decision. I will wait for your decision tomorrow morning."

She implored, "I would have been happy if you had agreed to meet Gurpreet at least once..."

Cutting her short, he said, "There is no such chance. If you wish to marry him, go and do it. However, I shall break all my ties with you and go back. For all practical purposes you will be dead for me."

Just while they were leaving, there was a call from Tanishk. He asked, "*Chacha*, my parents say that you need not purchase anything for marriage purposes. Let us just have a simple marriage and you can give us an amount equivalent to the expenses you would have made for the wedding."

Mr. Bajaj asked, "How much do you expect me to give you?"

He replied, "Nothing much, *chacha*. They wish that you should give us around one crore."

Mr. Bajaj stated, "Let me think over it, Tanishk. I will let you know by tomorrow morning."

"Sure," he said. "However, we shall come to see the girl only if you are willing for the same. Basically, my parents wish to take a decision in a week, since I have to rush back. I only have a fortnight of leave remaining with me. And there are many other persons who are only too willing to give us a blank check. But we chose your niece over others since she is beautiful."

Mr. Bajaj ended the conversation by saying, "I have to consult my family members. Give me some time. I will call you back tomorrow morning."

He later discussed with his wife, "The guy's demand has further increased. What should I do?"

She expressed, "Look here! If she does not get married,

we are complete losers. Ten-twenty lakhs here and there is not important if you look at the larger goals."

He said, "He is saying that we should have a simple marriage, but tell me how can I? It is also a matter of my reputation. And then, everyone will say that I did not take care of my niece. It means that I will have to spend around ten lakh extra for the wedding arrangements. And who knows what he will do with the money. What if he simply vanishes?"

She stated, "It is very simple. Make a draft or a Traveller's cheque in the name of Monika and not him."

He said, "Oh! Darling, you are a genius! Yes, that is what I am going to do. Tomorrow morning, I will convey to him our decision."

She expressed, "I hope that your darling niece agrees to the proposal!"

He replied, "Yes, she will! She is a rather emotional person and I am sure that she will fall in line sooner or later. Though, I feel that Gurpreet is a rather nice option for Shipra, since both of them will stay in Patiala only and he is doing rather well."

She exclaimed, "You are a gem, dear husband! With one arrow, we have fired two shots and we will have two preys! Wow!"

□

14
A Marriage is Settled

Monika kept tossing and turning in her bed the entire night. On one hand was her love and security offered by Gurpreet and on the other, it was the affection of *chacha*. At one moment, she wished to run to Gurpreet and resign herself to the haven of his arms. At another instant, she wanted to follow *chacha's* desire. After all, he had spent so many of his years to be along with her to give her some company. He had taken care of her when the entire world ditched her. 'Only if I could go and meet Gurpreet and discuss with him my problems! He will surely have some solution! He always has!' she thought.

In the morning, after breakfast, she decided to go and meet him. While she was getting ready, *chachi* came and asked, "Where are you going, dear?"

She replied frankly, "Before taking a decision, I wish to go and meet Gurpreet. We have been together for long and had planned our life together. How can I arrive at a conclusion without consulting him?"

Chachi replied, "Okay. Do as you want, but take Shipra along. We will honour your decision, though your *chacha* has given his word. But it does not matter. What you have promised to him is very important."

She stated with moist eyes, "It is not like that, *chachi*! Please understand my condition…"

Chachi stated, "Alright. You have my wishes. Come back within an hour."

Gurpreet waited for long for Monika to call him. However, when she didn't, he thought that things weren't as bad at Monika's house as they had expected. He proceeded for the marriage of his close friend in Ambala, along with his family.

When Monika reached Gurpreet's home, she was stunned to see it locked. Where was Gurpreet at the moment she needed him the most? She tried to contact him on her mobile. However, the voice kept screaming in her ears, 'The mobile is switched off. She proceeded to Resham's house, hoping that she might be aware about his whereabouts, but she did not know either. With Shipra for her company, Monika could not really tell Resham anything. They returned home empty-handed.

Sensing something was wrong with Monika, Resham tried to connect with Gurpreet on mobile. However, it remained unreachable. Finally, she sent him a message asking him to contact Monika at the earliest.

Monika spent her time thinking of the dilemma in front of her. Her predicament was threatening her, coercing her and squeezing out her blood. It left her numb and dumbfounded.

In the evening, when *chachi* came and said, "Get ready! The guy is about to come to see you and meet you. I did permit you to meet Gurpreet, despite your *chacha's* stiff resistance. But now, I won't listen to any word of opposition or antagonism. Hope you understand that."

She waited to see Monika's reaction, but she remained silent. After all, she had no option. *Chachi* further added, "Wear this lime-coloured *chikan* embroidery sari which I specifically purchased for you for the day. And I have called the beautician for your makeup. Do co-operate with her."

Her mind revolted. Couldn't *chachi* handle the entire thing a bit diplomatically? Why did she have to be so blunt? She had never ever worn a sari before. Moreover, there was a bit of hostility in her. Why should she wear a sari? Even if

Gurpreet was not there in her life and a guy had come to see her, she would not have draped a sari of all the things!

She decided that she will not let things be so easy for *chachi* and *chacha.* She did not wear the sari but wore an off-white *salwar* suit instead. That too was just a normal one which she always wore at home; not the one her *chachi* would have preferred. She did not put up any makeup despite Shipra's insistence. The beautician waited for some time for her to change her mood, but then went away, seeing no change in her attitude. Since the guests had already arrived by that time, her *chachi* did not say anything. She must have also been afraid of Monika's opposition.

She could hear a lot of noises coming from the guest room, but she was not interested. Taking Gurpreet's photo in her hands, she wondered where life was taking her. When Shipra came to call her, she went disinterestedly. Though she was asked to carry a tray of tea cups, she went empty handed. She was aware of the disgruntled glances, but she refused to bother herself about them. She hoped in the deepest corner of her mind that the ordeal would get over as soon as possible. She would then be free to marry the man of her choice.

However, she was stunned to hear the guy's mother say, "Won't it be better if Tanishk and Monika discussed things alone? The compatibility of the bride and the groom is so important these days!"

Left with no choice, she took Tanishk to his room. It was then that her glance fell upon the photograph of Gurpreet kept on the bed. She tried to quickly hide it, but he had already seen the photo by then. He asked, "Who is he?"

She looked at him for the first time to see whether she should lie about Gurpreet's identity or disclose it. She thought that his gaze was rather soothing and she replied, "He is the man I love."

"Oh! So I am an intruder?"

"Yes, you are!"

"I am so sorry to have come in between you two. My

parents are too keen on this marriage. They rather liked you and everyone in your house."

She remained quiet.

He asked, "What do you have against me?"

She questioned, "What do you have in favour of me?"

"The fact that my parents have liked a girl for the first time is the most important thing for me. And...and...I don't know if you have been informed...she is a guest on this earth for only a few days. It is her ardent desire that I get married before she takes a plunge into the other world," he replied.

She looked at him, wondering if she was indeed a bad person. She asked, "I already told you that I love someone else. How will you accept such a person as your wife?"

"Your past does not bother me if you are ready to forget it. I think I fell in love with you at the first glance. Who wouldn't like to marry a girl who is so beautiful and yet so fragile and down to earth? I leave the decision entirely to you. From my side, it is sure that I love you and wish to marry you. I would also like to let you know what my assets are. I work as Vice President (Finance) of Deere International. If I continue with my firm, I will get just one promotion, but they pay me well. I stay in Paris and have a three-bedroom apartment there. I also promise you that if you agree to marry me, never will I discuss anything about your past love affair," he stated candidly.

She remained seated on her bed after he had left. Things would have been so easy had he refused for the marriage. But here was a guy who was ready to marry her despite knowing her past. And he was her guardian's choice!

After Tanishk's family had left, his uncle summoned her to his room and asked, "So what have you thought? Honour your *chacha* and *chachi's* words or run away with that guy... what is his name?"

She replied, "He is Gurpreet and is a very decent fellow. Please speak about him with respect."

He said, "I don't believe in any formalities, but a secure future for my children is what I look for as an elder – be it you or Shipra. I don't find your future secure with Gurpreet. Anyway, you are allowed not to follow my advice. After all, who am I? Certainly, I am not your father, though I did try my best to follow his footsteps. I even shifted my whole home, disregarding Shipra and Ritesh's comfort and future. But, so what? You all are children of Gen Z and why should you bother about all these things? Anyway, I shall expect your answer by tomorrow morning since they wish to hold the engagement ceremony day after tomorrow in case we are interested."

She went back to check if there was any message from Gurpreet. There was none. There was a call or two from an unknown number, which did not interest her. What caught her attention was the flood of messages from Tanishk. Some were simple quotes on love, while others were philosophical messages. In the end, was a message which said, "I don't really think that you will marry me, but if you do, I will be the happiest man on the planet and shall respect you and love you till eternity." Angrily she took out the sim card from her mobile and angrily twisting it, threw it away from the window.

She again could not sleep that night. Confusion reigned in her mind. When her uncle called her in the morning, she had finally made up her mind. She told him without emotions, "I am ready to do as you have suggested." It was a different thing that she went and wept a lot in front of her father's photograph.

Varun Bajaj was ecstatic. He called his wife and said, "We are only inches away from achieving our aim. Co-operate the way you have done till now and we will have got what we desired. Monika has agreed for the marriage."

She said, "Have I ever not co-operated? I know that you mean well for me and our children. I will do my best. I am as ambitious as you are."

□

15

Gurpreet's Rendezvous

Gurpreet was a sought-after guy. For long, he did not realise that his mobile had no signals since he got lost in the din of the marriage party. He was a soft spoken, handsome looking and a fast rising businessman who hailed from a good family and almost every other person had a daughter whom they wanted to be married to him.

Though most of the proposals were received quite subtly, one aunt, who called herself Laveena, was blunt enough to call her daughter and said, "Monali, this is Gurpreet from Patiala. Why don't you both talk a little? Who knows...something, something may brew up between you two!" She winked at both of them and vanished from there, taking away everyone else who was present there, saying, "You know, we should stay away when two youngsters talk. It is so awkward for them..."

Gurpreet looked sceptically at Monali, who was all the more at unease – albeit for a different reason. Dressed in a pink Patiala *salwar* suit which twinkled a lot, she had put on a lot of pink lipstick and a big round pink *bindi* which looked larger than her forehead. Holding her long tightly-tied plait in her hand, she kept playing with it. He could very well understand that she was trying to be coy, which was not really her personality. They both stood there for a long while without uttering a single word. She smiled every now and then, looking at him, which he found very funny. Finally, to break the ice, he said, "Are you studying or working, Monali?"

She cackled and said, "Good girls don't work, *ji.* I am waiting for marriage, *ji.*"

The only thing which he felt for her was pity. How could a girl spend her life thus? Monika's reflection shone in his eyes and he smiled. Suddenly, he started hiccupping. The pupils in Monali's eyes went round and round as she said, "I will get you some water, *ji.* I think someone is remembering you!"

The moment Monali was gone, he ran away from there. Finding no place where he could spend some moments in isolation, he went to the confines of his car. Seeing him go away from her daughter, Laveena Aunty rushed to him, but he took out his mobile and feigned as if he was on an important call. She waited for some time and then went away.

Only after she had gone did he remember that he had not received any call on his mobile since long and checked it. It was then that he noticed that the mobile had no signals! He switched off his mobile and restarted it. However, the signal was still missing. He went to the nearest booth to call Monika. When she did not take the call, he assumed that everything was fine and relaxed.

While he was returning back from the booth, seeing him perturbed, his mother called him and asked, "Any news from Monika?"

However, by that time, another aunty joined in the conversation. Introducing herself, she began, "I had been waiting since long to see you both together. I am related to Roopam and I had seen your son at their house. Earlier I did not approach you thinking that they are going steady. The youngsters today fix their marriages on their own and have no respect for their tradition. Anyway, I am happy to know that you and I do not have a family belonging to those kind. I have come to you to ask for the hand of your son for my daughter, Tarika. She is an absolute beauty. And then, we have no issues regarding dowry. You name the amount and it will be yours.

My husband earns a lot and there is no dearth of money in our house. Being the only daughter, everything belongs to her after all. Anyway, let me introduce you to Tarika."

Finally, when she stopped and went to get her daughter, Gurpreet said angrily to his mother, "I am already troubled and this is something I do not wish. Since the time I have come here, everyone wishes me to be their son-in-law. From now on, we are not going to attend any marriage and this is my final decision."

She replied, "Yes, I can understand your distress. But I could not have refused to come for this marriage and you know why."

He said, "Yeah, don't I know that? Dr. Khosla was the person who saved your life. Coming for his daughter's marriage was warranted by all means. But how do I endure this Aunty *ji* who speaks nonsensically and without waiting for any reactions?"

Just at that moment, his glance fell upon Laveena Aunty who was returning with Monali. "Oh God!" he said in disgust.

"What happened?" asked his mother.

"You have another could-be daughter-in-law coming over. Take care," he replied and sped away from there, only to be asked by Dr. Khosla to run some errands for him, which he did happily. He loved being of some use, but he despised these girl-wallahs, trying to win him over by hook or by crook. He also pitied them in a way, since he understood how difficult it really was for parents to get their daughters married. But he certainly was not an answer to everyone's worries.

After he had arranged the extra rooms in the hotel, as desired by Dr. Khosla, he went to him to inform that the work was done and ask if he could be of any other use. Dr. Khosla replied, "Oh, yes! Do go to the groom's family and just ask them if they are comfortable. Be with them and just try to do whatever is best."

He asked his father to accompany him. He knocked at the groom's chamber and introduced himself. The groom also shook hands with him and replied, "Hi, I am Angad! Pleased to meet you!"

Angad – the name immediately caught his attention and struck something in the chords of his memory. He wondered if he was the same Angad who once wished to marry Monika. He also remembered that this was the guy who had caused a lot of troubles in her household. He felt like asking Monika and as soon as he got some spare time, he called her again from the hotel's number. However, the call was not taken by Monika once again. He remembered that she had told her that there was something evil associated with the name and felt that Dr. Khosla was not correct in marrying his daughter to the man. He told about his misgivings to his father also, who calmed him by saying, "Gurpreet, there is no use saying anything at this point of time, unless we know something concrete, otherwise we will be branded as spoilsports, who wish to ruin the marriage. My suggestion to you is simply to forget everything."

Sumptuous snacks had been arranged for the bridegroom and other *baraatis* at the hotel by Dr. Khosla and as Gurpreet saw them enjoying the food, he was happy. At least, the part for which he was made responsible was being taken care of was being dealt properly. That is why he was surprised when Angad came to him and said, "Partner, the arrangements are not proper. Can you ask Dr. Khosla to come over?"

He asked, "Please let me know too, so that I can take care of it."

The groom replied, "A few of my relatives have sugar problems. There are hardly one or two sweets for them. For a person of my repute, wouldn't it have been better to have at least five or six sweets? If this is the way things are being handled before marriage, I wonder how it will be during and after marriage."

He was stunned. How could someone even think like this? He was outraged and would have had a fight with him, had his father not intervened and replied, "Don't worry, *beta*! The sweets will reach you in fifteen minutes. We are extremely sorry for the inconvenience."

When he came out with his father, he burst in anger, "What is this, *pitaji*?"

His father replied, "Your young blood will not understand a few things. Just don't worry about it. Go to the *mithai* shop and get things as asked. It is indeed a sham what we do in the name of tradition. But then, do we have any options in this case? We will never do such a hullabaloo in your marriage."

His marriage! It brought back the smile on his face once again! The memories of Monika were indeed very lovely. And how lucky he was that his parents were a good balance of tradition versus modernism! He could never tolerate such nonsense in his house and he wouldn't have to struggle for it thankfully!

□

16

Crossroads

The hardest thing for Monika was to inform Gurpreet about her decision. None of them had ever expected it or thought that they would have to compromise in love. They had had a peculiar love story. Initially, Monika had been completely unaware of Gurpreet's love for her and had thought of it as an impossible thing. Later, she had miraculously fallen in love with him and they had begun thinking and dreaming of their life together. Even in the wildest of their dreams they had not expected that they would have to separate. But then, life is strange. Destiny is full of twists and turns and it chose to part them as she watched helplessly. She was not sure how she would break the news to him. But she had to. She owed him truthfulness at least, if nothing else.

Monika wanted to inform him as soon as possible. While she was dressing up, Shipra came into her room and asked with a twinkle in her eyes, "Where are you going? Has *jeejaji* called you to meet somewhere?"

She replied with disinterest, "That is none of your business."

No sooner than Shipra had left the room, her *chachi* came inside and embracing her, asked, "I can see that you are so happy that you have decided to dress up well. I am so happy for you."

Monika replied, "*Chachi*, I am going to meet Gurpreet. I have to inform him about the change in plans."

Chachi removed her arms from around Monika and said, "You can't do this, Monika! It will create a scandal. What if your husband comes to know that you went to meet another guy even after the marriage was fixed? We will be thrown out of the society. This is simply not done."

She replied hesitatingly, "But I did tell Tanishk about my affair with Gurpreet and he understood. It is obvious that I will have to tell him. I did everything as per your choice; at least let me inform him in my own manner."

Chachi said, "The first mistake you did was to inform Tanishk about your affair. It is a rather silly thing to do. Still, if you so strongly wish to inform him, I will come with you to his house. I don't want our family to be disgraced."

She pleaded, "Alright, at least let me appraise Resham."

Chachi said, "I don't think it is proper for you to leave the house. Better call her home," and left.

Monika felt as if she had been locked in her own house. She did not eat food that day. She cursed herself for having destroyed her sim card. Now, there was no way of connecting with Gurpreet. Of course, she had already made her decision, but she yearned to meet him and inform him herself about it and also explain him the circumstances which made her take that decision.

For long, she kept crying. After she had shed her tears, she opened her laptop and watched the photos which they had clicked together in their few years of courtship. Every snap brought loads of memory in front of her eyes, in which she was lost. How easily they had become a part of each other's life! So satisfying were their moments together. None of them ever had any undue expectations from each other, making their journey so smooth! When *chachi* came with a lot of *ghaghras* and saris, asking her what she wished to wear, she was least interested. She said, "I have no choice. Decide upon whatever you think is good."

Chachi enquired, "We have invited almost all the relatives and friends. Do you wish to call anyone?"

She replied without involvement, "No!" The only persons close to her were Gurpreet and Resham. Calling Gurpreet was out of question and she could not really get engaged in front of Resham. She knew her ins and outs and would have easily discovered that it was a decision forced upon her.

There had been no communication with Monika since the time he had left Patiala and this was making Gurpreet very anxious. All efforts to call her on mobile had been rendered futile. Since the time they had been together, there had not been a single day without any message from her. This was the only time he was unconnected and felt nervy. When he could control his nervousness, he rushed to Resham's house and informed her about it. Resham was also worried and she said, "I will go to her house and find out."

When Resham rang the doorbell, it was opened by Monika's *chachi* who looked overjoyed. Embracing her, she said, "Since long Monika wished to meet you and we were waiting for you to share our delight. *Beta*, I am so happy today! My eldest daughter, Monika is getting engaged tomorrow. You have to come for this important event."

"What?" she asked, "But, to whom?" Since she knew the story of Gurpreet and Monika's romance, she was taken by amazement.

Chachi replied, "That is a surprise. He is indeed one of the most handsome guys in the area and in our caste and is completely besotted by our dear Monika. And why not? After all, she is the best. I am proud to say that she is even more beautiful than Shipra!"

Resham did not utter a word. She was stunned and also a bit disturbed for Gurpreet. She liked him a lot and could not really digest the turn of events. *Chachi* guided her towards Monika's room and she followed her mutely.

On Monika's bed were spread a few colourful *lehengas* and saris. Seeing them, Resham was totally shocked and she asked Monika crossly, "How and when did this happen? Did you not have time to even inform us?"

To Monika, her anger seemed justifiable. She herself had not fully reconciled to the decision despite having taken it herself. She had a feeling that she was being compelled to take the decision and this only increased her dislike. Her confinement at her house was something which was making her all the more rebellious. She was happy that Resham had come home. She could at least shed a few tears on her shoulders!

But even that was not to be, for *chachi* did not leave the room even for a split second. In her presence, both the friends were quiet and it was *chachi* who was doing all the talking. Finally, Resham got up and said, "Monika, I am leaving."

Words failed Monika and she remained silent even then. She was too much overpowered by guilt for having ditched Gurpreet and despise for her *chachi*. It was *chachi* who went to leave Resham. After they had left, Monika felt that she could bear it no more. She was disturbed a lot. Never had she failed anyone, leave alone chucking someone. She was a girl who always honoured every word that came out from her mouth, just like her late father. Everything that was occurring was against her wish and she felt helpless. She went to the kitchen to fetch a glass of water. Her gaze went on a Swiss knife kept on the top shelf of the cupboard. She took it and carefully hid it under her clothes. She crossed Shipra on the way, and she let her pass by giving her a smile. The moment she was in the confines of her room, she locked it properly. She opened the sharpest knife and slit her wrist. She saw blood oozing out almost as water flows out from a pipe in the garden. She thought of Gurpreet and uttering his name umpteen number of times, closed her eyes. Slowly, she could feel losing her consciousness. It was not that she did not wish to live. She had survived the worst ordeal of her life and she was brave. She did cry a lot when her family members died, but she never gave up. She had felt her father say during those times to pull on. Her father, despite his death, had always been around her, guiding her, encouraging her and giving her the zest to live. He had been absent since two days. She was sure that it was because he disliked what was happening. Her father stood for truthfulness and loyalty. But she was a betrayer and a betrayer had no right to live. She felt a violet light surrounding her and engulfing her till she was a prisoner. She struggled to come out of the violet bars, but she could not. The more she tussled, the more inside she was pushed. And then everything disappeared. Everything was dark. Now she was afraid, extremely afraid. She struggled for some time. Soon, the energy began failing her. She wanted to run, but she couldn't. She wanted to push the darkness with her hands, but she could not find her hands. The faces of Gurpreet and her father appeared in quick succession in front of her eyes and then, she collapsed. Two hands came and supported her. She held them tightly and clung to the figure.

□

17

The Road not Taken

Tanishk had come to visit his would-be-bride casually just to see if everything was alright. He knocked on her room gently at first and then slightly strongly. When the door was still not opened, he called Ritesh and together they broke open the door. They were shocked to see Monika lying on the carpet, amidst a pool of blood. He immediately called the hospital services, who promised to send the ambulance along with a doctor. Ritesh had alerted everyone in the family and all of them gathered there. The moments were spent in extreme agony and distress.

As promised, the ambulance appeared within a few minutes. The Bajajs were quite well known and a senior doctor had come over, who took Monika under his charge. He stated, "Quite a lot of blood has been lost. Just pray that we are able to save her."

Mr. Varun Bajaj was a very troubled man. All his efforts seemed to have come to a naught with Monika's suicide attempt. His reputation, which he had slowly built since his brother's death seemed to be wiped away in a split second! If only he had been more careful!

While Monika was rushed into the operation theatre, everyone else waited outside, full of nervousness. Mr. Bajaj had summoned the best doctors from Chandigarh, but then, one could only try. It is God who decides.

After three hours of struggle, when the doctor came out and finally said, "Things look better now," that they finally relaxed.

By next day, Monika was slightly better and was shifted to a private cabin. At that time, only Tanishk was present and he helped her settle down in the room. When she opened her eyes, she saw that he was holding her hands. However, she was so weak that she slept off again. When she opened her eyes once more, he was still holding her hands. The kind gesture did not fail to touch her heart and she asked, "Why are you here?"

He replied, "Because I love you."

She paused for a few minutes before she said, "But..." She could not continue the sentence and left it incomplete.

He said, "Were you going to tell me that you love someone else? Yes, I know that. You already told me. I realised how much you love him when you took this extreme step. I still can't understand what made you do this. I had already explained you that if you decide to choose him, I shall be alright with it. May be, my selfish love for you did not let you explain it properly and I am extremely sorry for it. I love you, but my love is not so greedy. I am ready to remain unmarried for you my entire life."

She sobbed again – this time to her heart's content. She felt better soon. He patted her head till she slept again.

When she got up, he was still there. He said, "I was thinking of calling Gurpreet, if you permit."

She stared blankly at him. How could he be so generous? She neither refused nor welcomed the idea and chose to remain quiet. Tanishk went outside for a few minutes and then came and sat again with her, trying to make her laugh with his silly jokes. A few minutes later, she saw Gurpreet enter the room and she wanted to hide herself. She just could not face him.

Tanishk and Gurpreet shook hands and then Tanishk left the room.

Gurpreet stared at her and then, as if in an impulse, imparted a kiss on the back of her right palm. He questioned her, "Why, Monika, why?"

She sobbed and said, "I just could not help it, Gurpreet. I am a person who honours her words. I was caught between my duty and love and found it tough to balance the two."

He kneeled on the ground so that his eyes were at the same level as hers. He said, "I am not asking about that. Duty always comes before love. Even if you had told me, I would have tried my best to convince your guardians, but if they were adamant, I would have asked you to go ahead. What I want to know is why did you become so weak? Suicide is a path adopted by those who lack strength. I am sure that a girl I love can't be so weak!"

She replied, "I didn't know how to face you."

He said, "I am sure that you must have tried your best to convince your guardians, isn't it? And you must have agreed to their suggestion only when you found no solution. I am no angel and I won't say that I was not hurt. I was totally devastated. However, our love is not physical. The world can stop the union of the bodies, but not that of the souls. Our souls are one and united."

She asked, "What do you want me to do?"

He stated, "Look, my parents are there in your house to meet your *chacha* and *chachi*. I am here, courtesy Tanishk and your *chacha* does not know it. If my parents are able to convince your guardians, it is the best. Otherwise..."

She asked, "What will we do otherwise?"

He could not reply her. The lecture he had practiced all the way suddenly appeared impossible to explain. He looked away from her.

She asked again, "What will we do otherwise, Gurpreet? I am asking you..."

Closing his eyes, he said, "Then we will learn to stay without each other."

She questioned, "You mean to say that I should get

married to Tanishk?"

He asked, "Do we have a choice?"

She said, "Let us run away, Gurpreet and start a fresh life somewhere."

He answered, "If this was possible...if this was a solution... then yes, I am willing. But, this is not a practical solution. What I can assure you is that if your guardians do not agree for our marriage, then I will remain unmarried."

Covering his mouth with her fingers, she said, "Please don't make such statements!"

He replied, "Whether I say or not, my decision is final. And, if you really love me, you have to promise me something."

She asked, "What?"

He said, "You will get married to Tanishk without any regrets."

She began crying again. He said, "And you will not shed a single tear. I have met him and I have talked to him. He seems to be a nice sort of guy, who is fond of you."

She caught him by his collar and kissing him once again, said, "Tell me that you don't love me. If you don't, then I will marry anyone you wish."

He replied, "I love you and you will marry the one whom your guardians choose despite that. Let us await the news my parents come up with. Listen, carefully Monika. I love you and shall love you till I die. If you ever need me, I will always be there for you. However, if destiny has something else in store for us, then be ready to face it."

She asked, "But...but...do you remember the moment when Shipra caught us in the car? Do you recollect what you had said? You had stated that you will be always there with me and will come with me to face the world. Where is your strength gone now?"

He said, "You don't understand, Monika! There is a lot of difference between the two situations. At that instant it was facing the consequence of our actions. At this particular moment, it is thinking right."

She questioned, "And do you think it is right to leave me?"

He replied, "Who am I to leave you? I want you forever. But the society does not want us together. And how correct you are! I am weak to face the society. I can't see people condemning you. I cannot bear someone pointing fingers at you. And then, you will be secure in the hands of Tanishk."

Just then, there was a knock at the door. Entering inside, Tanishk said, "I am sorry to intervene, but Monika's *chacha* just gave a call that he will be here in five minutes."

Monika watched Gurpreet go away in misery. She could not understand him. Nor could she comprehend Tanishk. On one hand he had himself called Gurpreet and on the other hand, he did not say that he will not marry Monika since she loved someone else. She craved to run to Gurpreet and say, 'Happen what may I am ready to be with you and spend my life with you forever and forever and forever.' But what if he rejected her? A sense of self-pity engulfed her. She was sure that Gurpreet was a coward and felt disgusted to have fallen in love with him. How did she ever trust him?

She knew for sure that her *chacha* and *chachi* would never permit her to get married to Gurpreet. She felt that a treachery had been played in her life. She again remembered her father. If only he was there!

□

18

Getting to Know Tanishk

Monika remained in the hospital approximately for a week. Her suicide attempt was carefully hidden and everyone was simply informed that she was admitted in the hospital due to appendicitis. During the period, Tanishk remained her constant companion, trying to cheer her up. He would say, "Monika, if you can't accept me as your fiance', I would be happy to be even known as your friend. Just trust me."

For different reasons, everyone wished the marriage to be held as soon as possible. It was therefore decided that the engagement as well as the marriage would be held the week thereafter.

In the midst of all this turmoil, Tanishk would come in her life like a fresh whiff of air – filling her with freshness. She had already told him about Gurpreet and he accepted his existence in her life. He even asked her about how and when she fell in love with Gurpreet, which made her feel at ease with him. She even shared a few anecdotes of her love story with him.

One day, she lay on her bed, pondering about her recent past, when Tanishk crept in her room silently. Unaware of his entry, she was still lost in her thoughts when he asked her, "Where is my sweetheart lost?"

She jumped up with a start and asked, "When did you come? I hadn't noticed..."

"Will you ever perceive my presence in your life? I am so charmed by you and your beloved presence, but you hardly seem to care. Will you never love me dear?" he questioned.

Asking him to sit down, she said, "I think, it is difficult for me to forget him. I don't wish to be dishonest with you."

He said with a sigh, "I understand. And I am ready to wait. Just that he came in your life before me, otherwise.... Anyway, even if I wish, I can't ask you to get married to him, for neither does he wish it that way, nor will your guardians support. I promise that I will not touch you till you desire me."

She wondered about the man. How could he be so loving and caring? It was sheer ill fortune that she could not marry the man she loved. However, it was plain luck that she was to marry a man who loved her. She decided to be more tolerant towards him. Hence, when he asked her out for a lunch, she did not refuse. He said, "Please wear the off-white *salwar* suit that you wore that day. I really adored you in that attire."

While he waited for her outside, she wore what he desired. She even put on a little nude coloured lip-stick after long. She put on off-white danglers in her ears, a chain on her neck and a white *bindi* on her forehead. She was not really doing all this for herself, but for him. She had disregarded him too much and he deserved at least a little attention. If she could not return his love, she could at least return his friendship.

He looked at her admiringly and said, "You are the most beautiful girl in the world and I am so proud to be marrying you. I am sure that one day, you too shall love me."

Instead of the restaurant in which they were supposed to go, when Tanishk turned his vehicle towards another direction, a shriek came out from her mouth, "Where are we going?"

He smiled, "You will see for yourself."

She panicked. She was just getting to know him and was not even that comfortable. Had it been Gurpreet, she would not have minded for she knew and had full faith. Her eyes remained watchful and flustered. She felt that his eyes were on her all the time. Finally, he asked, "Don't you believe me?"

She said, "I don't believe anyone. Please tell me where we are going."

He stated, "In marriage, it is very necessary for the two persons to believe each other. We require a blind faith in each other. Learn to believe me. I won't harm you. After all, I am a friend first."

Despite his assurance, she remained agitated in her mind. It was only when they reached the Tanishq showroom, did she calm down. After halting the car and before getting down, he said, "I will be happy if you believe me in future. I just wished to purchase a ring of your choice for you," and smiled.

Not being completely sure of what he wanted her to buy, she looked only for the ones which were not so costly. However, he said, "I want to give the best to my bride. I know that diamonds can't ever demonstrate my love for someone, but I will be happy to gift you something of your choice. After all, one gets married only once."

He made her check the solitaires in platinum. She really liked the stuff and chose one which looked delicate as well as sophisticated. Happy at her choice, he said, "I am so happy to discover that our choice in the first thing that we are purchasing together is the same. I really hope that it goes on in the same fashion in future!"

She questioned, "What if it doesn't?"

He chuckled, "There is something called space. I will always give you your space. I do hope you will give me mine."

She grinned. He seemed to be a nice person indeed. If not the best, he was certainly a close second.

He then said, "I want you to choose your attire for the marriage too. It is a tradition in our house to gift the bride her wardrobe." For a moment, her heart fluttered. She had dreamt of herself as a bride, but as a bride to Gurpreet. How could she go with someone else and choose apparel for the wedding? Then her mind explained to her, 'In the same way that you chose the ring.'

They went to the best showroom in the town. By this time

she had compromised in her mind. She told Tanishk, "I will wear whatever you wish."

Though he asked her again and again to choose, she could not. He asked her, "Would you like to wear a *lehenga* for the wedding?"

She nodded. He asked the shopkeeper to take out the best *lehengas*. When he saw that she was not choosing, he shortlisted four and said, "At least chose one of these now!"

She remained hesitant still. Though the purchase of ring had not shaken her so much, the purchase of clothes did. It was then she noticed that there was also a turquoise coloured *lehenga* among the shortlisted ones. She was terrified. She remembered the moments in which Gurpreet had said so often that he wished to see her in a turquoise colored *lehenga* during their wedding, which of course did not materialise and could never take place. Finally, when he chose that turquoise *lehenga* only, she screamed, "Any *lehenga,* but not turquoise coloured!"

Everyone around was taken aback by her sudden outburst. When Tanishk pressed her hand lightly, she realised her act which had raised so many eyebrows around. Tanishk said, "We will purchase the *lehenga* some other day."

When they had seated in the car once again, he asked, "What happened dear? Why this sudden flare-up?"

She remained quiet. However, when he persuaded her again, she finally did tell, "It reminded me of him."

He said, "It is alright. We will go to some other showroom tomorrow."

Later, when they went for their lunch, she was happy to notice that Tanishk took care to order things only after asking her. While he kept narrating her many incidents from his college days, she chose to remain quiet, though she did observe that he spoke well and kept her engrossed.

Finally, by the time he ordered an apple pie as a dessert for both of them, she had reconciled a bit and she also began to speak. However, what came out from her mouth were only incidents related to Gurpreet, which he listened with rapt attention. While narrating him one such incident, she was reminded of something funny and she chuckled loudly. She felt someone was watching her intently. And then she saw; it was Gurpreet. Their glance met and she froze. This certainly was not the time they should have met, but then it was a small town. Tanishk also followed her gaze and when he saw Gurpreet, he invited him over. Things were rather awkward for her. Here was a man whom she loved sitting with a man she was marrying and she was sandwiched between them. She had to make real efforts not to let her eyes drip tears, which she did when she was finally alone at home in the confines of her room.

□

19

Seeds of Doubt

While she was lost in the turmoil, *chachi* came inside her room one day and presented her a card. The figures in the card had been made by a very well-known artist. Decorated with gold dust, it was indeed a very expensive card; and yet, it did not interest her!

When *chachi* left, the realisation dawned upon her that she was actually getting married and that too to a man whom she had not yet begun to love! Her whole body trembled. A fear of the unknown gripped her being. In Gurpreet's case, she had felt very comfortable. After all, she knew all his ins and outs. And she also knew his family well.

The word family reminded her again of Tanishk. She had not met his family since the time they had come to see her. And when they were at her house, she had hardly interacted with them. She could not even recall their faces.

When Tanishk visited her in the evening, she asked him about his parents. He smiled and said, "I am so happy that you are finally showing some interest in me. My mother is having severe kidney problems and is on dialysis. In all probability, she won't even be able to make it for my marriage. I have been extremely upset since a few days, but she was equally insistent that I should get married. After all, she questions, God knows when I will get a chance to come to India next. The decision has been tough for me."

"Oh!" she said, "And I was so lost in myself that I never cared to ask you. Now, I remember that you did tell me about her ill health during our first meeting. Why don't you postpone the marriage?"

He replied with a twinkle in his eyes, "She wishes not only to see her daughter-in-law, but also her grandchild before she leaves the world."

The thought made her blush. He lifted her chin with the tip of his finger and said, "For the first time, I am seeing you so coy and, believe me, it suits you! Don't blush again, for you will make me fall in love with you once again." He hid her face in his shoulders and continued, "As such, I don't know why, I have a feeling that it is either now or never. I want you at any cost and I am afraid that if I leave you, you will never marry me."

She asked, "Shouldn't I go and visit her in that case?"

He suddenly released her from his embrace. She could see lines on his forehead. She looked at him properly for the first time since she had got to know him. He was a tall man, broad-shouldered and silken straight hair. His eyes looked like a mixture of blue and brown. In short, he was quite handsome to look at and any girl would have felt great to marry him. She began comparing Gurpreet and Tanishk. She closed her eyes. Both of them appeared in her mind, one after the other, in a cyclic pattern. However, it was still Gurpreet who occupied her heart. Love is indeed blind, she thought. Otherwise, why did her heart not permit her to love Tanishk?

Meanwhile, Tanishk's voice echoed around her, "I think my mother would be happy to meet you, but I suppose that there is a custom according to which the bride cannot visit her in-laws' house before marriage. I am not really sure if she will permit it."

She asked, "Do you believe a lot in customs and tradition?"

He replied, "Monika, I am staying abroad and naturally, I cannot follow it at all over there – though I have my own set of little rules. However, when I am in India, I try to abide by my parents' desires. After all, that is the only thing I can do for them. Anyway, I will ask her in the evening and confirm to you by tomorrow. If she permits, I shall be happy to take you. Otherwise, four days hence, I shall take you permanently."

That again raised the strands of her hair on her skin. Four days! She was afraid, genuinely afraid!

He asked, "Are you in a mood to come with me to purchase your *lehenga* today?"

She nodded. She really did not have a choice.

They went to a different store that day. Though mechanical, she began to take interest in the purchase. She noticed that the shopkeeper did not show even a green or blue *lehenga*, leave alone the turquoise one. Had Tanishk instructed him not to? She smiled. At least he was taking care of her little things. She should be happy, she told herself.

While they had shortlisted the *lehengas*, someone came and hit her loudly on her back. Who else other than Resham could do it? She happily turned around and both the friends hugged each other. When she introduced her to Tanishk, he immediately said, "Oh! This is such a lucky thing! Why don't you help us choose the bridal *lehenga*?"

A fuchsia coloured *lehenga* was finally chosen by the three of them. Asking the shopkeeper to make the *lehenga* ready, he addressed Resham, "Why don't you join us for a cup of coffee?"

Just after they had seated, there was a call on Tanishk's mobile and he went outside to take the call. Resham asked her in annoyance, "Why have you not been answering my calls? Even if you have decided to marry Tanishk and not Gurpreet, I remain your friend, don't I?"

She stated, "But, it was I who was wondering why you have not called and convinced myself that you didn't wish to maintain any contact with me in view of...but, when did you call?"

Resham replied, "I must have called you not less than ten times. Every time, it is either Shipra or *chachi* who would pick up the phone and tell me that you are not at home. Anyway, tell me how are you? Knowing you well, I was sure that you must be finding it difficult to adjust to the new circumstances and I thought I might be of help. Does Tanishk know about Gurpreet? Did you meet Gurpreet? He has gone out of station to some undisclosed location and I was worried."

After Monika had narrated to her the entire story right from her suicide and Gurpreet asking her to marry Tanishk, she said, "I find the entire thing rather unconvincing. If any guy knows that his sweetheart loves someone else, either he will break the relations with the girl or he will help the girl in finding her beloved."

Monika remained quiet. Resham continued, "And tell me one thing. What if you face problems after marriage? I haven't seen many guys taking it so nobly that his wife loved someone else. If I were in your situation, I would never let the two twain meet. Something looks fishy – very fishy."

Monika said, "I think it is your love for Gurpreet and my togetherness with him which is making you say all this. Tanishk seems like quite a good fellow. Though I don't love him, I have accepted him as my would-be husband. And I am sure that with the help and support that he is providing me, I will also love him eventually."

Resham remained pensive. Finally, handing over a chit to her, she said, "I don't know if I will get to meet you alone after this. This is Roopam's phone number. Yes, she is also in Paris, the place you are going to go. In case of any problems, contact her. And don't worry; she is a changed girl now. This reminds me, is your visa ready?"

"Visa?" asked Monika, "Well, I had never thought of that. I will have to ask either Tanishk or *chacha*."

They saw Tanishk returning. Resham whispered, "Just check how much dowry is involved in the marriage."

All three of them chatted for a little while. Tanishk was extremely courteous and charming towards Resham.

After Tanishk left her home, she confronted *chacha*, "Is there any dowry involved in my marriage?"

He looked thoughtfully at her and then sensing her anger, replied, "Not really! I have thought of gifting you a crore of rupees as a marriage gift though for your own needs. I am sure that you will never require it, but it shall remain with you in your name."

She bombarded him with the next question, "What about my visa? Am I supposed to stay back in India or go with him to Paris?"

He replied, "Don't you think I am more bothered about these questions than you? A visa cannot be made till you are married. I have made all other papers ready and we are only waiting for the marriage certificate. It is decided that while Tanishk will proceed immediately to Paris post marriage, you will stay back for a fortnight in which time your visa will be made ready."

The answers calmed her. The seeds of doubt that had been sown in her mind by Resham were taken care of. She smiled and said to herself, "This Resham is indeed very sweet! She loves me so much that she wants everything to be perfect. I am lucky to have a friend like her. Fortunately, everything seems fine; otherwise...I always have her."

□

20

New Concerns

After Monika had left, Poonam asked Varun, "Why did you tell a lie to Monika? Aren't we paying a huge amount as dowry? You could have scored on the front by telling her as well."

He replied, "It was only a partial lie. I did tell her that I am gifting her money. The only fact I concealed was that Tanishk had demanded it."

"And why that? I am sure you had your reasons..."

"Yes, I have! From what I have learnt about my niece, I know that she is an extremely sensitive creature. If she comes to know that the marriage was based on dowry, she may again retaliate and refuse to get married. Just like my late brother, she is a bit principled."

"What if she comes to know about it from someone else?"

"My dear wife! I do know what I am doing! Tanishk had requested me not to let anyone know about the dowry being gifted. Though he had cited different reasons, I do know the real one. He will not disclose."

"And what is that?"

"Don't you know how much these guys negotiate for dowry? I am sure that we were not the only family which was under their consideration zone! The highest bidder gets the guy and we were one. That is it! Marriage is no more a union of the soul; it is a market in which money plays the most important role."

"I often wonder what will happen when we begin looking for grooms for Shipra!"

"For her, we will have to spare more money. She is neither as beautiful as Monika nor does she have much brains."

"Hmm..."

"But that is why we are earning – to get Shipra married into a good family and to settle Ritesh."

"Hmm...you had suggested Gurpreet for Shipra the other day...shall we talk to them?"

"How silly can you be, Poonam? This is not the right time. Firstly, Monika and Gurpreet are still attached to each other. Secondly, I have already spent a lot and can't afford another marriage at present. Let Monika go to Paris and then, I will make such an offer to his father that he won't be able to resist. Money can buy everything. And the easiest thing to buy in our country is a groom, who gets sold by auction to the highest bidder."

Just then Shipra entered the room. She asked, "Were you both speaking about me?"

Varun smiled, "Ha, ha, ha! How did you guess?" Kissing her on her forehead, he said, "We will get the best groom for our dear daughter!" Then looking towards Poonam, he added, "I have to go to look after the arrangements for the marriage. The guests will pour in from tomorrow. I hope everything is set on the house front. Remember, there should be no mess. Everyone has to be well catered to. And yes, why don't you go to the market to get marriage gifts for all relatives and friends from our side?"

Poonam replied, "Yes, I remember that the task is still pending. It will be done today."

After Varun had left, Shipra sat down on the bed. Though Poonam was busy with her work, she had an intuition that there was something up her mind. She watched her as she kept twisting and turning her long plaits, chewing her nails and biting her lower lips. Finally, she burst, "*Maa*, I am not going to marry as per your choice. I am in love and I shall get married to the man I love."

She looked at her sharply and asked, "Who is your latest boyfriend? Don't I know you? Every month you get a new boyfriend and then dump him for someone else. Till when are you going to play these games? Aren't you weary of them? I have not yet told your father about your misdemeanours; wait till he gets to know them."

She was quiet, but only for a moment. Next instant, she erupted like a volcano, "You have pestered me enough by threatening me that you will tell papa. I don't care anymore. Do whatever you want. You will tell papa, *naa*? Go and tell. What have you both done for me? You only care for Monika and no one else. Ritesh and I have been treated as if we are not your children. What was it that made you both bring us here and forsake everything? I loved my city, I loved my friends and I loved my house. Why should I stay in someone else's house though I have one? And then, here also, we were nicely disregarded by you. It has been Monika all the while. May I ask why? Are you not our parents?"

For a moment, Poonam was stunned. Everything that she and Varun were doing was for their children's interest in mind. She didn't know that her own daughter harboured so much of revulsion in her mind. Patting her head, she said, "Shipra, everything that we did was for you and Ritesh. Can't you see what we were before coming here and what we have become? What was our standard before and where are we now? We had just a two-room flat and here we live in a bungalow. We could afford you no luxuries that time, and now you get the thing you name. What else do you desire?"

Shipra asked irately, "But did you ask us about your happiness? I think I was happier in my small house. I was satisfied without luxuries. From the moment we have arrived here, you and Papa have completely vanished from my life. I could never understand what it is after which you are running. I lost you the instant we left the house."

Poonam pleaded, "We have been securing your future, Shipra. Can't you see the money involved?"

Shipra yelled, "Money...money...money! Can't you see anything beyond money? I don't need your money, especially at the cost at which it has come. I hate your money and I hate you. And take it as a warning – a final one. I will only marry Shivam. He is the guy whom I had been waiting for since years. He is the guy who makes me feel good. He is the guy who makes me feel loved and wanted." Without waiting for a response, she got up and went away.

Poonam sat on the bed with a heavy heart. She always knew that something was wrong with Shipra, but she had never taken it seriously, thinking about it as a childhood immaturity. Now, she knew it was certainly more than that. She felt the edifice of her life crumbling. What she and Varun had so carefully planned right from the beginning was leading to nowhere. How could she explain to Shipra what all they had both endured to reach where they were today? Had they not done all this, their family would have gone to rags. Theirs was rags to riches story, thanks to Angad. But she could not even narrate the tale to her children. It was too dangerous to tell.

Just then, Monika entered the room. Seeing her desolate state, she began pressing her forehead. She said, "*Chachi*, I think you are over-exerting yourself. See, you look so tired! Why don't you share your work with us? I mean, I can't handle too many things, but I can surely run smaller errands!"

She looked at her lovingly for the first time. Here was a girl who loved her so much and worshipped them as God. What had they done to her? She ran her fingers in her hair. She said, "Let me get some lime water for you. I think you are exhausted."

A splurge of love emerged from her heart. She wished to cuddle Monika at that instant. However, the moment she left the room, Varun entered and the moment was gone. He had come to take her to invite the big shots of the city and she had to leave immediately.

After they sat in the car, she informed everything about Shipra to her husband who silenced her by saying, "Why do you get so carried away? These are small hiccups in the long race, but we shall win. Shipra is just being silly and I will tackle her after the marriage. Right now, we just have to concentrate on properly organising the marriage so that no one can raise any fingers at us. By the way, I find the behaviour of Tanishk very amusing. I had invited the page 3 photographers to capture the moments of the marriage and the photos were to be published. However, Tanishk sends a message that since his mother is not well, the marriage has to be kept low key and that no videos and photographs should be taken! We can't do that, can we? I have refused the page 3 fellows, but I will take out a few photographs at least."

□

21
Marriage

Soon the Bajaj house was full of clamour and clatter. Even far-flung relatives had come over and Poonam found it extremely difficult to manage things despite the horde of servants that she had. Each person had a particular taste and peculiar requests and they were always full of complaints.

Monika had not yet completely adjusted to the fact that she was getting married to someone other than Gurpreet. After the arrival of the guests, she sought more and more of solitude. She was sure that they had no love for her and had come for either some greed or formality and she let her *chacha* and *chachi* handle them. She missed Resham badly, but she knew her *chachi's* dislike for her and did not dare to invite her much.

Finally, it was the night just before her wedding day. She felt particularly unhappy and calamitous. She was having goosebumps! Would Tanishk remain as adoring as he was presenting himself to be? Would her in-laws accept her completely? How would his relatives be? How will she pass the fifteen days post marriage? How will her life in Paris be?

Again and again, her thoughts would fly off to Gurpreet. Their past was a treasure she had. She speculated whom he would get married to. When the mind drifts, it goes just anywhere. She was sort of jealous of his wife. She wondered if they would ever meet again. May be, when they meet, both of them would have their own kids!

She shuddered at the thought. She remembered that Tanishk had told her that he would not touch her till she desired, but will he maintain it? What if he forced himself upon her? After all, he would be her husband and had every right to demand it from her. She was extremely nervous and frightened. She drifted to sleep early in the morning. When her eyes opened, it was already 10 a.m. *Chachi* came along and said, "Get ready for the engagement. Tanishk has arrived."

Chachi had purchased a lime-coloured net sari with green border for her engagement. She helped her tie the sari. She decked her with the costliest of jewellery. The beautician further enhanced her beauty. Though she had no desire to look at herself, her *chachi* made her stand in front of the mirror and said, "Just see how pretty my daughter looks! You indeed are the best! Tanishk is a lucky guy to be marrying you."

When she went down, everyone looked at her in awe. Tanishk kept gazing at her adoringly and as a result, forgot that he was supposed to put the ring on her finger. Some cousin of hers shouted, "*Jeeju*, stop ogling at my *didi*. You will have her for yourself soon."

He blushed and apologised. Still gazing at her eyes, he slipped the ring on her ring finger. Soon, it was her turn. In him, she saw the image of Gurpreet. She wanted to run away. She looked around. More than a hundred eyes were on her. She closed her eyes and glided the ring on his finger. Everyone clapped. She had not yet opened her eyes. He pressed her palm gently. She finally opened them. He signalled as if to believe him, after which she finally normalised.

The function was over. She was officially tied to him for life. Another formality of marriage remained which was to take place in another eight hours. She shuddered.

However, after that she had no time to think. She was surrounded by someone or the other continuously. And then, there were so many rituals to be followed. The *haldi* ceremony was held soon after. As soon as she had taken bath, the beautician asked everyone to go out of the room and said, "For full bridal makeup, I will take at least three hours. I don't want anyone here."

Monika felt that she had become a machine which was being decorated and embellished without her consent, ready to be presented to her husband.

By the time she was ready, it was already quite late and most of the guests had already left for the venue. Only Shipra and one of her friends remained. She looked at her and said, "You are very beautiful, but you were my biggest enemy. I am so happy that you will soon be gone. I don't wish to see you ever again."

Monika was miffed. She asked her, "But, what did I do to make you a foe? I suppose, we hardly ever spoke and our paths never really crossed..."

She replied haughtily, "Your money was the greatest distress. It pulled my parents towards you. And you made the best use of it."

Monika decided to remain quiet. As far as she remembered, *chacha* and *chachi* had themselves stated that they wished to stay back with her. Not that she disliked it; she was really happy with it. Had she been alone, she would not have known to handle herself, leave alone the vast business empire. She was, therefore, grateful to them. But she had never wished that it should be at the cost of Shipra or anyone else.

Just then there was a call on Shipra's mobile and she said, "My mother wishes that we should hurry up since the auspicious time for the marriage is in an hour."

There were no shy steps she should be taking. Shipra or her friend did not even hold her hands as is generally the case. Alone she walked for her own marriage, with Shipra and her friend following her as if she did not exist for them. When they reached the venue, she saw Resham also reaching at the same time. They hugged each other and she accosted her to the *mandap*, where Tanishk was waiting for her. The garlands were soon interchanged. Everyone clapped and flowers were thrown at them. Tanishk pressed her hand lightly and smiled at her. Coyly, she looked around. She thought that she should touch the feet of her in-laws. However, she could not find them around. She wanted to ask someone around. Her *chachi* was busy welcoming guests. She was not comfortable asking Tanishk. Brides were, supposed to remain quiet. She voiced her concerns to Resham, who assured her that she would find out.

However, people swarmed up the stage at that very moment to present gifts to the couple. She could not really connect to the guests and there was awkwardness in her gait. The only thing that worried her was that all relatives were either her parent's friends or her *chacha's* friends or their relatives. There was no one from Tanishk's side and she was disturbed. Meanwhile, she saw that Resham had come back. However, the presence of people around made it difficult for both of them to talk. Finally, the last of guests seemed to have presented gifts to the couple and they were left alone. She asked Tanishk forthrightly, "Tanishk, I can't find your parents or any relatives for the marriage..."

He replied with a grim face, "Yes, Monika! Everything is known to your *chacha*. Unfortunately, my mother had to be flown to Mumbai for her kidney condition. She is still battling between life and death. Had she not promised me to get married, I would have postponed everything. You must not have heard about a person who gets married when his mother is struggling."

She stated, "But...this is not done...you should have told me. I...I feel so bad about this...oh...anyway, let us go to Mumbai just after marriage..."

He replied, "Let us see. I have to fly to Paris day-after-tomorrow. I think I will go alone to Mumbai."

She asked, "But why? Now that we are already married, I am a family member too – isn't it? I mean, the *feras* will be over soon..."

He said, "It is a difficult city to stay in, Monika. For you, managing things there will be difficult. Anyway, let us watch her condition. If it deteriorates, then we will be left with no other option."

A few more guests came to the stage with gifts and their discussion got interrupted. And it was then that her gaze fell upon him. He was sitting silently on a chair at the further end of the *mandap*, sipping a cold drink. His gait looked as if he was extremely tired and grievous. For a moment, she was angry at him. It was because of him that she was sitting on the stage as someone else's bride. Otherwise, they would be happily married somewhere. Only if he had a little guts.... Only if he was not a coward.... Only if he was a man enough....

They were summoned for the *feras*. Even while she was taking rounds, her glance now and then fell upon him. She wondered why she could not really dedicate herself to Tanishk and the events taking place. Was the past really so difficult to forget?

□

22
Learning to Love

The crowd was thinning out. However, Gurpreet had not yet come to meet the bride and groom on the stage and this troubled Monika. When she glanced again at him, she saw him towards the area earmarked for a bar. But he never drank! How was it that he was heading towards the bar? She saw him make a peg for himself and she was terrified. Gurpreet had begun drinking! For a moment, she wished to go to him and ask him to throw it away. But, how could she? She was now a wife of someone else and all such privileges no longer belonged to her.

She was so lost in her own thoughts that she did not see a few young lads come towards the stage in a tipsy condition. They were singing aloud cheap numbers and seemed intoxicated. One of them approached her and said, "*Parjai, ek dance ho jaaye*! You are a *maal*!"

She looked towards Tanishk, who told them, "Come, let us go and talk somewhere. You are not going to do this."

They had some discussions and the guys were silent for some time. She asked him, "Who are they? They look rather boisterous and cheap. How do you know them?"

He looked a bit nervous as he said, "Don't worry dear! I will take care of them!"

She asked, "But, who are they?"

Before he could reply, he was summoned by *chacha* to meet someone and he went down. The very next moment, those guys came on the stage again and began troubling her with their nasty and cheap comments. She looked around for help, but when she saw no one around, she tried to climb down the stairs. One of them caught her hand and said, "You belong to all of us, *parjai*! How can you go?"

She struggled to free herself, but she suddenly saw him on the stage, taking command. He hit the person who had held her hand so hard that he was blue in fear. By that time, everyone had seen the pandemonium and reached the stage. While *chacha* talked to Gurpreet and the guys, Tanishk took her aside and said, "They are my distant relatives. They will create a lot of problems for me and especially, my mother if they are treated badly. Can you please ask Gurpreet to apologise?"

She replied, "How can I ask Gurpreet to apologise when he is not wrong? Let those relatives of yours go to dogs and I don't care. Do you know what they were telling me?"

He asked her strongly, but intently, "He will have to apologise. Why don't you understand? Otherwise... otherwise..."

She asked, "Otherwise, what?"

He replied, "How and what can I tell you everything just now? Please ask him to," and then added in a rough voice, "otherwise, you will have to bear the repercussions. You are newly married and you don't understand anything."

No one had spoken to her so rudely in her entire life. She was flabbergasted. By that time, *chacha* had left them and was coming towards her. She expected some relief from him. However, she was shocked when he said, "That friend of yours, does he not know how to behave? Is this the way the relatives of bridegroom are handled?"

Tears flowed from her eyes unremittingly and she made no effort to stop them. Wiping her tears, she proceeded towards Gurpreet and calling him aside, said, "Gurpreet, I have no right to ask you, but if for old time sake you can apologise to those bastards, it...it would be great."

Gurpreet looked at her, shocked! He went to those people and said, "I am sorry." Then he glanced at her again, as if wishing to say something, but decided otherwise and went away. As she watched him go, all she wanted was to go and hug him tight and say, 'Please take me away from all this to a land where only you and I exist, where there is only love and where there is only happiness.' However, she could not. As she observed him go, she felt that her own shadow was going away. She wondered if what was happening was correct. Her mind screamed and replied, 'No, nothing seems to be correct... nothing at all...and nothing is going to be correct. If only...if only I had forced Gurpreet, reminded him of his vows and done something...may be, I should have approached his parents... may be...' However, life passes on. She could not undo what was done. She had to face what was written in her fate.

Tanishk sat down on the sofa once again, gesturing her to sit too. She sat reluctantly. His relatives had gone away by then. He said strongly to her, "Now that we are married, it will be nice if you sever your ties with your old flame. I don't want you to meet him and...that is an order. I have heard a lot about him, but now I can take it no more. Enough is enough."

She was certainly not used to being commanded. All she wished to say was 'go to hell', but she glanced around. There were a lot of people still around. She chose to remain quiet.

Chachi came along with a few other ladies to accost the couple for dinner. Monika was in no mood to eat. She had seen the side of Tanishk which she dreaded. Even if Gurpreet had not been in her life, she would have never thought of marrying such a person. She had been brought up in a very delicate manner and she was still very fragile despite her having braved so many incidents in her life.

After all the guests from outside had left, they were taken into a room to relax. A few younger cousins joined them for some fun and teased the two of them. However, all she yearned for was space in which she could freely shed her tears. She was so lost that she did not see that her cousins had left and only the two of them remained. She noticed it only when he kneeled in front of her and said, "I am so sorry to have hurt you, Monika. I can't really explain to you how perplexed I was! They were relatives from my father's side and we sort of...we don't get along well. I did not know how else to diffuse the situation. He has never really cared for my mother and...and I was afraid that his anger may get aggravated again and...I am so sorry for my misbehaviour."

Nice that she was, she set aside her own annoyance and said, "Oh! I am so sorry to know. But, shouldn't you have explained earlier? It sounded so cheap that time..."

He lowered his head and said, "I understand dear! You can't imagine what I had to go through to be able to ask you to tell Gurpreet to apologise. I can't even raise my head in front of you."

She said, "Alright! Let us forget the incident."

He stood up and taking her in his arms said, "It is my good luck that you not only agreed to marry me, but also have forgiven me and my actions." Kissing her, he continued, "We only have a few moments together. After that, I will be leaving for Mumbai and then Paris. I will be in touch with you and try my best to get your visa so that you can join me as soon as possible. I am looking ahead to a quiet and peaceful life with you in Paris. I have a three-room apartment in Paris, which I had started renovating before I came to India. I believe it is ready."

She asked, "Where shall I stay till then?"

He replied, "Why? With your *chacha*, of course!"

She said, "Normally, after marriage, no girl stays in her maternal house. I don't wish to stay there."

He stated, "I feel so bad, but we have no choice. My parents are in Mumbai and you can't possibly go there. Neither can you accompany me without a visa. And what is there in a fortnight? It will pass in the wink of an eye."

She protested again, "I don't wish to. I am no longer comfortable in the house."

He asked, "Why dear? It is your own house, isn't it?"

She replied, "Officially, yes. It is my house since in my father's will, it was gifted to me. But since *chacha* looked after me like a father, neither shall I ask him for it, not shall I assume that it belongs to me. Let it remain under *chacha's* care."

He asked, "All that is between you I suppose. I hope he did gift you something."

She enquired, "Gift me something? Why, he made the entire arrangement for the wedding..."

He said, "Monika, I should not interfere since all this is between you and him. But he did tell me that he would be gifting us...I mean you, an amount of a crore..."

She replied, "He did mention to me something about it. Since I am reaching you after fifteen days, it is quite possible that he will give me later. But, why does it bother you? You are not looking at it as a dowry, I am sure..."

He stated, "Hey Monika! How can you ever think like that? I earn well and am at a respectable position. I don't need your money at all. It would be a shame on me if I have to use your money. I just asked to understand if everything is alright at your end."

□

23

The Longing

Tanishk asked Monika, "Will you please close your eyes, dear?"

She asked, "And why?"

He said, "Please close them for a moment..."

After she shut her eyes, she felt his fingers around her neck. A few moments later, he said, "Now, open them!"

She saw a necklace of several solitaires around her neck. She looked at it in amazement. He said, "I want the best for my sweetheart, since I love you. I will make all efforts for it, but do excuse me in case I fail anywhere. Ours is a lifelong commitment now, isn't it?"

The necklace meant a lot for her. It was not the money, but the feelings. He had indeed been trying his best to please her since she had met him. She smiled. He kissed her again and took her in his embrace. She melted under his charismatic arms. The thought of Gurpreet once again arose. But she thwarted all their attempts to make their appearance and closed them in a box of pleasant memories deciding that she will never ever open it again. Soon, their bodies entwined and they were one.

Their bodies were as tired as their mind, since it had been a hectic day and both of them dozed off. When Monika arose, he was already awake and smiled at her. Taking her in his arms once again, he said, "You are the most beautiful woman I have ever known. You have a heart of gold. I am indeed extremely lucky to have you as my wife."

She said, "You are stating as if you are going somewhere."

He laughed, "Of course, I am! The time has come for me to depart. *Chacha* and *chachi* will be here anytime to take you home. We shall remain connected and I shall try my best to fly you to me as soon as possible."

She got up hastily. He gazed at her and smiled. It was a naughty smile, but they had no time for any mischief. She winked at him. They kissed up hurriedly once again. Just then, there was a knock on the door. Her *chacha* and *chachi* had arrived.

The time for separation had approached. All of them went to Chandigarh to leave Tanishk from where he had to take his flight. While they approached the airport, she wondered about the changes in her life. A day ago, she disliked Tanishk and was marrying him only because she was asked or rather coerced to. And now, she was already missing him. She wondered how marriage transforms things in the flicker of an eye.

After they had left him, they returned back. In the comfort of her room, she lay on her bed and thought about her life whose clippings ran in front of her eyes like a film. So much had changed in the last few days. She was an already married woman now and not a carefree girl anymore. She decided to do things which would make Tanishk proud of her as his wife.

Monika was a unique girl. Till then, she hardly visited internet much, despite her entire generation remaining hooked on to it. However, it being the need of the hour, she began learning to use it. After all, she desired to know more about Paris. Till then, she had been completely unaware about the world. She thought that English is an internationally spoken language, used everywhere. When she learnt that many Frenchmen did not know English, she decided to learn French and enrolled herself with the only tutorial teaching French. Of course, she did not inform Tanishk about it. After all, it would be best to surprise him. Till then, it was he who had chased her. Now, she wanted him to know that she loved and cared for him too. These were simple ways in which she thought that she could.

The French classes were only for an hour a day and that too only three days a week. However, she wanted to learn fast. She also had very less time. She requested her French teacher, Ms. Raksha, to give her more hours. Seeing her dedication, the teacher agreed and her classes were held three hours a day and she got busy with that.

True to his words, Tanishk telephoned her at least twice a day, which pleased her. It sounded good that she had someone who was genuinely worried about her. It had been years since she had seen that kind of love. Gurpreet also loved her, but then, there was a difference. He was just someone whom she loved; Tanishk was someone who not only loved her, but was also her husband.

One day, when he called her, he said, "Monika darling, my house is almost ready and is waiting only for your arrival – almost like I yearn and crave. I have been staying here since long and it never looked so dull and lonely to me, as it does now. Only the kitchen needs to be renovated and then the house will be completely geared up for your arrival."

She replied, "I am also waiting every day for the visa to be granted. Do you think I am enjoying here?"

He laughed and said, "I hope not! Monika, life is so different here. You are used to staying in a bungalow, but here there are only apartments – one building with many flats. Almost all the persons staying in our building are Europeans. One flat has a Sri Lankan couple and I love visiting them. His wife makes wonderful tea. And we also have a Pakistani, who cooks really well. He has also just got married and his wife will join us in a few days. Hope you will adjust here. And I want to tell you one more thing – it is almost impossible to get a servant here. You are so much used to servants, but despite earning so much, I can't afford it. I really wish I could."

She replied, "For love, one can change ways. Since the servants are so easily available here in India, we have them. But I suppose, working won't be so much of an issue with me. After all, I have you!"

He stated, "Yes, I wanted to tell you that I am a good cook. I never even entered the kitchen when I was in India, but I learnt the labour of work only here. Once you come, I will cook for you the most lavish dishes."

She stated, "It would be my pleasure...but, why will you cook? I can make everything for you...."

He laughed, "Why are you so much like a typical Indian wife? If you see here, everything is done on equal footing. We both are the same..."

She also giggled at the statement. He asked, "Now, why are you laughing? Of course, there are things which only you can do, such as bearing children...but I can surely help you in other things..."

Children! She smiled. When she thought of it again while sleeping, she loved the idea. She even began contemplating how her children would look like. She loved the thought of a little girl. She could even imagine how her daughter would be – a combination of little shyness and naughtiness. She wondered how Tanishk will take up the responsibility of a father. She could see him smilingly take up the job of changing nappies and giving her a bath.

Monika longed to be with him as soon as possible. When there was a delay of a week in the formalities of her visa, she felt forlorn. The only thing which gave her solace was that she had learnt French enough to speak well. Her teacher was extremely happy with her progress. She told her, "Had you waited to give the exam, you would have topped."

She grinned, "I hope to top in my exam at Paris."

Her teacher said, "I am sure you will. Your husband will be amazed to see that you can speak French so well and that you learnt it in such a less time!"

Finally, when the time came for her to leave, she was full

of glee. She was happy that she would finally have her own house. Though both Shipra and she had avoided each other's company since their last encounter, she felt unwelcome in her own house despite her *chachi's* affection.

Her *chacha* and *chachi* came to leave her till Delhi. Once she entered the Indira Gandhi International Terminal, she felt small in front of its majestic size. However, she was happy that she was leaving Patiala and was on her way to Paris, the place where her solace lay. Never for a moment was she afraid of what lay ahead – even when she took her seat on the flight. She was flying for the first time, but there were no goosebumps. And should there be? After all, Tanishk was waiting for her. She also looked ahead for spending a wonderful life with him.

□

24
To Paris

It was Monika's first journey by plane. She was certainly not used to sitting on one chair for hours together. Initially, there was the excitement of flying, but as time flew; it changed into disgust and then despair. She was surrounded by eerie people around and this aggravated her problems all the more. She had an aisle seat and the couple sitting next to her had twin sons, who kept on yelling all the time as a result of which she could not even sleep. The only solace was that she would meet Tanishk at the end of the journey. And whenever she thought of him, she forgot all her despair.

She had read so much about Paris that she thought that she knew the city already. She had a desire to see all the spots of importance. She wondered if Tanishk would think that she was foolish if she told him that she wished to see De Louvre so much. And then, she smiled. She was sure that he was a wonderful person and would love to take her around.

She had got the novel titled *Da Vinci Code* and she got engrossed in reading it. She had specially chosen this title since it was based in Paris and her desire to see all the fascinating spots further mounted. Finally, when the plane was about to reach Paris, unknowingly she dozed off. When the lady sitting next to her tried to wake her up, she was irritated thinking that her children wish to go to the loo once more. When she noticed that the plane had already landed, she woke up with a start and switched on her mobile. At that very instant her mobile buzzed. Tanishk welcomed her, "Darling, I am so happy that your feet have blessed my city! Welcome to the majestic city of Paris! I am impatiently waiting for you just outside the departure gate."

She blushed; she had everything in life that any girl could wish for. The airport at Paris was huge, and had she not known that Tanishk was waiting for her, she would have been terrified by its mammoth size. It had many escalators to take care of the long distances, but she was slightly afraid of them and did not use them. Though she walked very fast by her own standards, she found that she was still lacking behind the Europeans who were much taller than her and walked with longer paces. Her mobile buzzed once again. "Hey, where are you? Why are you taking so much time?" he asked. She loved this continuous attention.

When she finally reached the exit, she was extremely delighted to be with Tanishk once again. They hugged each other and he began kissing her. There were already so many people in and around them that she was embarrassed and moving out of his embrace, said, "Why are you publicly disgracing me? What will everyone think?"

He laughed and replied, "This is not Patiala, Madam! Welcome to the land of Paris where everything is fair in love and war! Tomorrow I shall take you to visit the city around and you will be surprised to see many couples smooching and kissing and going even ahead..."

She said irately, "The place may have changed, but not the persons. We are the same. I am happy to follow my Indian tradition with which I feel connected. These foreign traditions do not interest me."

Putting his right hand over her waist, he said, "Come on, let's go. Don't worry, I will not ask you to do anything that you don't like." She relaxed after that and the lines of tension which had appeared on her forehead disappeared.

He took her to a silver-coloured Mercedes and dumped her luggage behind. When she saw the car, she was surprised to find that the steering wheel was on the left hand side, unlike that in India where it is on the right hand side. Though she had read so much about Paris, she was amazed to find how different things were practically as against theory. That she would find many more such things which would shock her was not known to her at that point of time.

She did not really relish when she was asked to put on the seat-belt, but she understood. The drive was rather interesting. She had read on the net that the city had wonderful architecture, but then, it is said that seeing is believing. She loved every bit of it and was so engrossed in looking outside that she did not even notice that Tanishk had asked her something. When he tapped her on her shoulders, she was brought back into the world. He teased her, "Monika, the charm of Paris has made you forget even me, isn't it?"

She replied, "How can I forget you? You are a part and parcel of life. The charm of Paris shall fade with time. But not yours!"

He stopped the car on the side of a road and looking at her unbelievingly, asked, "Monika, since when have you become romantic? It was I who was chasing you all the while in Patiala, while you showed almost no interest. And now, you speak so lovingly? I can't believe it!" He planted a light peck on her cheek.

She asked innocently, "Does it mean that since I have begun to love you, you will make me suffer?"

He cackled once again. But since he did not reply, she asked again, "Tell me, naa! Will you no longer be interested in me?"

He replied, "From where do you get such silly ideas? I loved you and shall love you forever. Even after you become a mother! Even after you grow old and have no teeth!"

She blushed and said, "I will always have teeth!"

He laughed once again. After almost forty-five minutes of

driving, they reached a hotel. She read the name of the hotel as 'Paris Marriott Hotel Champs-Elysees'. Tanishk asked, "Get down, darling, what are you waiting for?"

She replied with hesitation, "This is a hotel and not your apartment. Why have we come here?"

He smiled at her and said, "Just follow me for now and I will explain to you. I had thought of telling you on the way itself, but you were so immersed in viewing Paris that I decided to tell you in the room itself."

A man came to take their luggage inside. When they entered the reception area, she was amazed to see the grandeur of the hotel. It appeared to be a five-star hotel. Asking her to sit on the sofa, he went to the receptionist. She thought she was too miniscule in front of the magnificence of the hotel and lowered her head. When she heard someone ask, "From India?" she did not know what to say. She looked blankly at the lady who had questioned her. The lady asked again, "Are you from India?"

She simply nodded her head, while the lady continued, "As you must have guessed, I am also from India. I am Susy and I am a journalist. I am here for some official purpose. And you?"

Just then she saw Tanishk approaching them and decided not to speak to her. She got up and went to him. Looking at Susy, he asked, "Who was she?"

She replied, "I don't know. She was trying to be friendly with me, but I was afraid and didn't talk."

Holding her by the waste, he said, "That is better. This is a foreign land and you don't know about anyone. I'd prefer you don't speak to any unknown person. You will have plenty of company when we shift into our apartment and I will introduce you to pretty good people."

The room was also quite ostentatious and she asked him, "What is the cost of this room?"

He smiled and said, "It is seven hundred pounds a day. It is one of the grandest suites."

She enquired, "Why are we here? Why are you spending so much?"

He replied, "Well, the issue was, as I had told you a few days earlier, that while the whole apartment is ready, the kitchen still remains to be renovated and we surely can't shift to the house without a kitchen, can we? What happened was that I spent a lot of money on my mother's operation and was short of money. I applied for a loan and it should be sanctioned soon. Till then, I thought of welcoming you in style. You deserve everything! Even if I was asked to lay my life for you, I am ready."

Burying her head in his arms, she said, "Oh, Tanishk! How can you love me so much! I love you a lot. Let us shift to a simple room which we can afford."

Pressing her head gently against his chest, he said, "I have already booked this room for a week. We will shift to a smaller hotel after that. I am indeed blessed to have you in my life."

□

25

A Fresh Beginning

They chatted for a little while. When he got a call, and he remained busy with that for some time, she unknowingly drifted into sleep. When she woke up, she realised that it had been almost twenty hours! She got up with a start and said, "Oh! I am so sorry!"

He was writing something, sitting on the study table and he said, "This is jet lag. I tried to wake you up so many times for food, but you were in a semiconscious state and I decided not to pester you."

She looked at her clothes and exclaimed, "I suppose I was wearing something else when I dozed off!"

He smiled wickedly and said, "Who do you think can change it other than me?"

Their gaze was locked for some time and she coyly shifted her glance. He came to her and collecting her in his arms, said, "Darling, let us have some food. I am so hungry!"

She asked, "But, didn't you have your lunch and dinner?"

He replied, "It was alright till I was alone. How could I have it without you since you are here?" Then, handing her the menu card, he asked her to choose and order. She turned the pages of the menu card several times and then finally said, "I don't think we should have food here. It is too damn expensive."

He laughed again and said, "When someone comes from India for the first time, he or she always finds everything expensive. It is all in the mind, since we convert it into rupees. I earn money in Euros and there is no need for you to be thrifty. I am sorry about the apartment, but I know I will manage it soon."

When she chose the dishes, they were all vegetarian ones. He asked, "Don't you take non-vegetarian food?"

She replied, "No! Why?"

He said, "It is very difficult to survive with vegetarian food in Europe, especially when you go outside. Why don't you take non-vegetarian food, by the way?"

She replied, "I don't know. I think because my parents never took."

He said, "You are so sweet," and then ordered some chicken dishes for himself.

While she was cleaning her teeth, she wondered why indeed she did not eat non-vegetarian food. She could find no reason. And then she thought, 'Why not try? After all, I have to stay with Tanishk now and since he eats it, it will be better if I too join him.'

Just after she had taken a bath, there was a knock on the door, indicating that the food had arrived. Only when she sat down to have food that she realised how hungry she was! Initially she had her vegetarian *biryani* that she had ordered, which she finished in less than two minutes. Afterwards, when she took a morsel of the chicken dish ordered by him, he looked at her astonishingly. She did not quite like the taste of the dish, but did not find it detestable also. 'May be, I will begin loving it with time as I have started loving Tanishk,' she thought.

He stated, "My office has been kind enough to grant me a week's leave, despite my remaining absent the entire month for my marriage. The leave has been specially granted to show my wife in and around Paris. So where does my wife wish to go today? Let us take a sightseeing bus which will take us around and give you a good idea of the city!"

She immediately replied, "No, I wish to go to Notre Dame de Paris today. I want to see the city from the Cathedral Towers."

He asked, "Then why not go to Eiffel Tower? It is located much higher..."

She replied, "You don't understand. It is also the architecture of Notre Dame de Paris which attracts me. Do you know that it took more than a hundred years to build it? And do you know that the entire city contributed in its making in some way or the other?"

He said, "All this goes off my head and I am not much interested. After all, I am a finance person. But yes, I am very much interested in being with you and seeing you smile. So, let us go!"

While they were getting ready, she remembered something and said, "Tanishk, I also wish to meet one of my friends in Paris."

He looked at her wide-eyed and asked, "Do you have a friend here? How come?"

She replied, "Do you remember Resham, my friend in Patiala? She is her sister."

He said, "That sounds interesting! It is nice that you will have some company here. Does she work here?"

She stated, "Yes, she works as a teacher. But that is just because she had some idle time for herself. Her husband is normally busy with his job and he wanted her to do something."

He asked, "Where does her husband work?"

She replied, "He works for the Government of India. More than that, I can't recall – though Resham did tell me."

He stated, "That sounds great. Let us do one thing. Let us visit them after our honeymoon period."

She blushed at the mention of the word 'honeymoon'. He cuddled her and planted a kiss on her lips. One thing followed the next and all thoughts of going out were postponed as they made passionate love.

After around two hours, when they untangled, Tanishk

asked her once again, "So, do you wish to go to Notre Dame de Paris?"

She reddened once again and he said teasingly, "Monika darling, get dressed and let us go before I take you once again in my arms."

Monika was mesmerised on seeing the facade of Notre Dame de Paris. How tall the structure was! The chimes and the clocks particularly attracted her. They even went to the Cathedral Tower by climbing all the 387 steps. The climb somehow made her feel that it was a place most suitable for shooting a movie. She herself felt like a movie star with her chivalrous hubby making her believe that she was on the top of the world.

By the time they were climbing down the steps, they realised that it was already dark. They walked near the River Seine to reach a small Indian restaurant which Tanishk knew offered some genuine Indian food.

In totality, Monika felt quite satisfied. When she lay on Tanishk's arms at night to sleep, it eluded her. For a moment, she felt as if she was in Gurpreet's arms. She had dreamt of this heaven only with him. She wondered how his thoughts still crossed her mind. After all, he was a long-forgotten episode of life. She commanded her mind, 'I don't wish you to even think of Gurpreet. He has ditched me. He could have married me. Now you have to think of only and solely Tanishk for he is my life.' She kissed him on his chest and smiled. He lay fast asleep.

When she woke up, it was already noon. She searched for Tanishk, but he was not in the room and she panicked. She felt helpless. She was alone in a foreign country with no one else other than Tanishk who knew her. She wondered why she had not felt worried while flying to Paris. So many things could have happened that time too; but she had been so carefree. She wondered what had changed in this one day and she could not find anything else other than a lot of love being showered upon her. Then why was she feeling so helpless, she pondered.

After a little while, a key was inserted in the hole and

Tanishk entered the room. She clung to him and said, "Tanishk, please promise that you will never leave me alone like this and vanish?"

He stared at her as if reflecting upon something and then asked, "What happened darling? I was and am yours. Can anyone leave such a beautiful and loving person as you?"

She replied, "You did," and lying down on the bed, began to sob loudly. Sitting down near her, he asked, "What happened all of a sudden, Monika?"

She said, "Neither do you know anything nor do you wish to understand anything. Didn't my father and my family leave me? Didn't Gurpreet leave me? Now you will leave me too."

Stroking her head gently, he said, "Not everyone is like that, Monika. And then, we are married, aren't we? The relationship is said to work for seven lives."

She was consoled after a little while and then said, "I don't know what happened to me. I think being alone triggered some subconscious nerves."

He cackled and said, "It is alright dear. Let us go out after having some quick breakfast. I am sure that you will forget all this and your grievous mood. Get ready, fast!"

□

26

Getting Acquainted

Monika wondered what she should wear and finally decided on a plain silk sari, turquoise in colour. After all, he had said that he did love turquoise colour and the desire to impress him was pertinent at that point of time. However, as he saw her drape the sari, he said a bit loudly, "What are you wearing? This is no apparel to put on in Paris. You can be really disgusting at times! Wear something which is worn by everyone here. Haven't you heard the saying, when in Rome do as the Romans do?"

She asked, "Why, what is the harm in wearing a sari? It is our national attire!"

He said, "Ufff...why can't you women understand? I am sick of this. You are a stubborn girl."

She questioned innocently, "And how many women in sari have you taken around?"

He replied distastefully, "Alright, wear whatever you wish."

His revulsion to sari made her wear it all the more. She told him, "I will wear whatever I wish to and you should not oppose. Remember, you used to talk about giving me space? Where is the space gone now?"

He said, "Alright! I surrender to you, Madame!"

While they had just come out of the room, they saw Susy

coming from the other end. Seeing her, she gave an admiring look and exclaimed, "My God! So dazzling you look in a sari! I can't believe it!"

She smiled back. However, her smile was constricted knowing fully well that neither did Tanishk like the sari nor the lady called Susy. Unaware of her turmoil, Susy continued, "Can I take a photograph of the two of you? You are a smart and handsome couple I should say and I'd like to capture you through my lens!" Without waiting for their reply, she began giving them a few instructions on where they should stand so that the photo that came out was a good one.

Monika saw that despite disliking to the core of his heart, he complied with her instructions. When she asked him to smile, he even grinned. However, the moment she was gone, he was red with anger and said, "We are not going anywhere. Let us go back to the hotel."

Seeing the frown on his face, she acted in accordance with his desire, though she could find nothing wrong in the entire episode. Tanishk remained busy on his laptop after that. She lay on the bed for quite some time, wondering what was so wrong. If he despised it so much, he should not have agreed for the photo at all. Finally, she decided to call a truce. For, after all, whom did she have other than him? *Chacha* and *chachi* had also not called her up since she arrived in Paris.

She walked towards him and said, "I am sorry for everything."

He looked at her and said, "It is fine," and continued with his work. She stood there for some time. He said crossly, "Didn't you hear that I said it is fine? Now let me concentrate on my work."

She just could not comprehend what he wanted. She turned about and ran towards her bed. Burying her head in the pillow, she cried to her heart's content. She heard him get up and walk away from the room. She felt helpless and destitute. She slowly drifted into a world of sleep. In her dreams, she met Gurpreet again. He calmed her down by stroking her hair and said, "Even though I shall not be near you physically for some time, I am always there with you." She also wished to hold him tight and hug him. However, when she tried to catch him, he was gone. She got up bewildered. There was a magazine lying on the centre table. She picked it up and turned a few pages. However, her mind was not yet stable. She changed her sari and wore denim and a tee. She peeped into the mirror. She didn't like her appearance. She had grown up wearing *salwar* suits and she felt that she was imprisoned in the denims. It was not that she disliked people wearing them; it was just that she did not like them on herself.

Just then, there was a click on the door and he came in. This time, he appeared to be in a better mood. He said, "I am sorry. I really don't like people interfering with my privacy. I am not a people's man and that is all. But I should not have behaved the way I did. After all, we are only growing to know each other. We will understand each other slowly."

He kissed her. She was reluctant initially but when he tried to gather her in his arms, she soon melted. Taking out two tickets from his pocket, he said, "Let us go out dear. I have got two tickets of hop-on hop-off bus. We will see the city by night on the bus."

She asked, "What is this bus?"

He replied, "Basically, the buses have fixed stops and come in a frequency of a few minutes. You can hop off at any of the stops you desire and then catch the next bus of the same company. It is quite an interesting concept and you will get an idea of what you wish to see later."

She soon got lost in the grandeur of the city once again as it took them to various nooks and corners. Paris was much more active at night and she was amazed to see the vivacity of the town.

At one of the spots near the Opera, after they had eaten some ice-cream, he said, "Well, this stop happens to be quite near our apartment. Would you like to go and glance at the building?"

She replied, "Why glance? I wish to visit the flat and see inside. I also desire to meet the Sri Lankan lady who makes wonderful tea and the Pakistani who recently got married."

He stated, "That is really sweet of you. However, we have two problems. Firstly, I didn't get the key of the apartment since I had not really thought of taking you there. Hence, we can't go inside. And secondly, no one goes to another's house unannounced in Europe. Certainly, not the way we do in India – going and knocking at anyone's house. It is always pre-planned. Even if a mother is visiting her son, she calls him and informs him. Hence, we will visit them some other day."

They reached a tall building which had around thirty floors. It was painted in white with stripes of grey. He disclosed further, "Here, we don't have a security man quite unlike India and the entire security is electronic. Hence, we can't even go up to the apartment without a key. However, this is our building which will soon be our house."

She found the entire system unbelievable. But then, it was quite possible. The novels she had read did speak about the formalities which were termed as good behaviour. She said, "I am not quite satisfied with this visit, but I have at least seen the building. What is its exact location?"

He laughed and stated, "You ask too many questions, don't you?"

She said, "Hey, why do you find my questioning so distasteful? What if I get lost somewhere and you are not there? How will I find my way back?"

He grinned again and said, "Don't worry! I do comprehend that you are new to the city and I will show you all the important landmarks. That is the reason why I am taking you on this conducted tour."

They caught hold of the bus again after a little time. Monika found the concept rather fascinating. They could see what they wished to and skip what they didn't feel like seeing.

While they were crossing the Arc de Triomphe, she said, "It looks so much like Gateway of India!"

He stated, "Indeed. The concept is the same."

She said, "I wish to come here tomorrow."

He smiled and replied, "Of course, we shall! Your wish is my command Madame." The manner in which he stated this made her smile too. 'How easy life is,' she thought as they reached their room once again. He asked, "Haven't *chacha* or *chachi* called you?"

She replied, "No, they haven't?"

He asked, "Do you wish to talk?"

When she did not reply, he connected the call. Her discussion with *chacha* was only a formality she thought. She rather felt more connected to *chachi* who asked her several questions including how Tanishk was treating her. Her enquiries were just as any other mother and she felt happy to be connected to her. She also asked her about Shipra and Ritesh and finally kept the phone down when she noticed that she had spoken for almost half an hour. She looked at Tanishk, wondering if he was angry. However, his face gleamed and was full of naughtiness, which she understood only too well by now.

□

27
Fairytale

Monika felt that the days were flying; the days were like a dream. She was growing to understand Tanishk and had adapted herself accordingly. She knew that he didn't like her talking to anyone and she avoided that. She understood that he did not like traditional dresses and she stopped wearing them. Life moved silently and yet fondly after that.

On her third day in Paris, he took her to see Arc de Triomphe and the nearby spots, as she had desired. This happened to be very near their hotel and they walked towards it in the morning. She was lost in the Napoleon's era as she recollected that he had ordered its construction and entered with his wife Marie-Louise with a wooden mock-up constructed. She felt like the Duchess Marie-Lousie entering with her husband Napoleon and she smiled. When he asked her for the story behind her smile, she blushed. He said, "For this smile of yours, I can do anything. Let us eat something and then take a ride on the boat and see the city from a different angle."

She was in love with the idea. After all, she had heard so much about River Seine! Initially, she had thought that the river would be as large as Ganges back home. She had not really believed that it indeed was River Seine. She wanted to see more of it. She had become much more carefree with Tanishk since the time she had come to Paris. She didn't mind anymore if he gave her a peck on cheeks or lips. She had comprehended that people did not really care about what the others were doing. Of course, she could never be as carefree as the people around, but her levels of comfort had shifted and this was adored by Tanishk. He often teased her, "You have graduated from a child to a woman!"

As they crossed the various monuments and places of importance in their boat, she was amazed. She wondered if she was indeed in heaven. Lovely were the moments and wonderful the company. Happiness and sanguinity dripped from everywhere.

The next day, they were to go to Versailles Palace. He said, "Before we visit the Palace, why not have a quick view of my office? It is on the way..."

She said grudgingly, "I don't want to see your office. My entire life, I have to see that only. I want to go to Versailles."

He stated, "Darling, you should know where your husband works, shouldn't you? It is important for any woman."

She said, "Not for me! I am least interested!"

He asked her, "Would you like to take up a job after you settle down? It seems like a good idea."

She replied, "At least at present, I don't feel like working. I just want to cook for you, take care of you and..." She left her sentence unsaid and her face flushed.

He questioned, "And?"

She said, "And have a dozen kids...." She ran away from him and hid her head under a pillow. He laughed, "A dozen kids? No *baba*! Then you will have no time for me."

It was finally decided that they would just have a glance at his office from outside, since they would be late otherwise for their next haunt. While driving to Versailles, he stopped in a corner. The huge premises of Deere International, the firm where Tanishk worked, was on the other side of the road. The tallest building was made of glass and it looked stupendous. She said, "You are indeed lucky to be working with such a firm.

And then, you are the vice-president! How lucky I am!"

He grinned, "I am so delighted to see you happy. The entire struggle which I went through to reach this level seems to have borne fruit. I too am blessed to have you as my life."

The tour to Versailles was marvellous. He floored her with his love and chivalry. Finally, it ended in her paying more attention to him rather than the place they had come to see.

On the fifth day, he said, "We have not yet been to visit the majestic lady. Don't you wish to meet her?"

She asked, "Majestic lady? Who is she?"

He cackled again and replied, "Arrey! The Eiffel Tower is also known as the 'majestic lady'. People from all over the world come to visit it and you haven't yet expressed your desire to go there!"

She replied, "Yes! Let us go there today!"

The queue to the entrance of Eiffel Tower was very long. However, even waiting with Tanishk was not an issue at all. He kept her interest alive with his interesting narration of various events. More than that was his sense of humour, which she had seen only lately. To surpass all these was his romantic talk, which kept her floored.

While they were lost in their conversation, a lady wearing a sari came to them to sell key chains of Eiffel Tower. She was too surprised to see an Indian selling such trifle things. It reminded her of Patiala where beggars and people selling everything, right from jewellery to pirated books, would pester them whenever their car halted on any square; or of the persons who would flock outside the temples and *gurudwaras*. She asked him, "How do I see an Indian selling such petty things here?"

It was not him who replied, but another lady in front of her. She had not really noticed the lady till then. She was also an Indian and Monika was pleased to hear her speak Hindi. The lady said, "These are the ladies who have either been abandoned by their husbands after marriage or those who have come illegally here."

She thanked the stranger for the information and chatted with her for a little while. She did see that Tanishk was cross again, but she had got used to it by then and didn't pay much attention to it. They were both mostly quiet after that. She knew what exactly was troubling his mind and decided that if he really loved her, he had to get rid of this. It was basic etiquette to talk a little if someone chats with you. And she was silent because it worried her. She was a very sensitive person. She wondered about the women who were abandoned by their husbands in a foreign country with no one to look forward for help. She wanted to do something for them. Only a day before Tanishk had asked her if she wished to work. She surely did not wish to work at this point of time, but decided to do something for such women in her spare time in future.

It took more than an hour for the serpentine queue to finally move ahead. However, when they got inside and climbed up the lift, she felt that everything was worth it. They indeed were at the top of the world!

Monika felt that she was in a dream. Watching the city from a height of over 100 feet was indeed mindboggling. She yelled his name from there and everyone around looked at her in disbelief. But she was past caring about people's reactions. She did what she pleased. Soon, Tanishk also joined her and they both shouted and shrieked in delight.

They spent more than two hours there without realising how time flew. After that, he said, "Monika, let us have lunch now and then just walk around to pass time. When it is dark, the tower twinkles and looks beautiful."

He took her to Trocadero from where the view of Eiffel Tower looked amazing. Kissing her, he said, "A kiss with Eiffel Tower in the background is considered eternal and the most romantic thing to do. Darling, our love is so sublime, so pure. In this city of love, kissing you is like taking another vow of everlasting love. I am yours forever and forever and forever...."

Pure joy emanated from his lips that moment. She also wished to seal the moment so that it lasted forever and forever.

That was the day she realised that she was completely in love with him. She had completely forgotten Gurpreet. Tanishk's love had a charm just like him. Little by little, he made her completely surrender to him and his love. Even the absence of her parents from her life seemed to fade in the background. She felt secure and safe in the haven of his arms.

There were a lot of benches on the platform and they sat there, arm in arm. He looked at her adoringly and said, "Your presence makes me feel that I am on cloud nine. You bring out the best in me."

She replied, "We are one now. And we shall always be there for each other in good or bad and in happiness or pain."

Before they knew, they had embraced each other and stayed in that position for long.

□

28
Sheer Joy

After they had dinner, Tanishk suggested, “Hey! Have you enjoyed night life anytime?”

She shook her head and added, “I have no interest either.”

He said, “One should see everything. Even if one does not enjoy, one should know. Let us do one thing – let us go the Le Lido show. It is a very interesting show with the Blue Bell girls.”

She stated, “I find night life disgusting.”

He chuckled and added, “It is not like the night shows in India. People here are very decent and they don’t ogle at every girl they come across. I am sure you will enjoy. And then, we can always come back if you don’t enjoy.”

Reluctantly, she agreed to go. On the way, she asked, “What happened to the loan? Was it sanctioned?”

He replied, “Unfortunately, no! Not, yet. I am so sorry that everything is getting delayed. If it had not been for my mother...”

She thought and suggested, “Your mother deserved what you did. After all, she is the one who made you. We can find some other way to tackle this problem.”

He said, “I really can’t think of any other option, dear! The only source of my earning is my job and though I earn pretty well, it will take at least a year to save for our kitchen. I am thinking of taking an apartment on rent and I did talk to an agent. He will show us a few apartments tomorrow."

She was pensive for some time and then said, "*Chacha* had given me quite a huge amount. I suppose, we can use it for the renovation. Why go and stay in a hired apartment when we have one?"

He kissed her immediately and said, "Oh! What a brilliant idea! But...I am rather hesitant...the money belongs to you and not me!"

She smiled and added, "We are husband and wife and the money belongs to both of us. Once we reach the hotel, I will give you the cheques and we can encash them tomorrow."

Holding her hand, he said, "Monika, I will return every pie that belongs to you. Just give me one year. It is really unmanly to accept money from your wife..."

She kissed him back and uttered, "It is alright if your wife willingly gives it."

He put his arm around her as they watched the show. While listening to one of the songs, she began humming with it. He was surprised and said, "How did you know this song? It is in French!"

She replied, "I was about to tell you, but there was no apt occasion. I learnt French in the days I spent at home after our marriage?"

"What?" he asked, perplexed.

She kept vibrating with the song. He again kissed her and said, "You perplex me, dear! How can you love someone so much?"

She replied, "We Indian girls are like that only. If we love someone, we love completely and are ready to do anything for the person."

Looking in her eyes, he said, "Yes; that I can see!"

She rather enjoyed the show despite her initial reluctance to go. Tanishk was correct in saying that people there did not ogle at the girls. The girls were respected as artistes. She was undergoing a cultural change and while she did dislike a few things, she adored most of the things. 'Thank God! I am here with an open mind!' she murmured, almost to herself. He asked her, "What did you say?"

She replied with a chuckle, "I said that I love you!"

He said, "Oh! I understood! Let us go back to the hotel."

Once they entered their room, they made passionate love. Slowly and slowly, all her opposition as well as inhibitions were waning and she enjoyed every bit of him and his love.

Though Tanishk was a late riser, he woke up rather early the next day and this astonished her. She asked, "Darling, I suppose you need more sleep! We had slept very late yesterday, hadn't we?" Memories of their lovemaking were in the back of her mind and she had turned pink.

He said, "Yes! I should! But I should also go and withdraw money for the renovation of our house. Till when will we stay in hotels like this?"

She stated, "Why are you always worried about something or the other? Why don't you leave yourself free for a little while and enjoy? As such, you will join your office in a day or two and we will not get time to enjoy like this."

He gazed at her face and asked, "Oh! So my babe wishes to enjoy?"

One thing led to the other and they made love again. After that, they both dozed off unknowingly. Monika was the first to get up and waking him up, said, "Hey, Tanishk! We are getting late for Disneyland!"

He got up with a start and said, "Oh! How could I sleep? I need to withdraw money first. Work is worship."

She replied mischievously, "I am not giving you the cheques till you take me to Disneyland! I want to enjoy the rides there."

Though he agreed and they were soon moving towards it, she felt that his mind was elsewhere and asked, "Did I do something to offend you?"

He replied, "Of course not! You are the best thing to happen in my life."

However, he remained mostly silent on the entire journey. By then, Monika had become used to his mood swings and understood that he did love her a lot and did not try to pester him with her doubts. She rather decided to leave herself completely free and enjoy. She immersed herself in the Hindi romantic songs which she had asked him to play.

Once they reached Disneyland, she first went to the musical tour where the multicultural dolls sang 'It's a small world!' Indeed, the world was small! She had flown from Patiala to Paris and yet, things were not much different. She had not found it very tough to adjust to her new world. Soon, their house would be renovated and they would shift into that to start a new life.

She loved the Space Mountain ride. Going into the unknown on a warp-speed ride was something she had begun to enjoy. Tanishk had expressed his unwillingness to join her on the ride and she had gone all alone on it. She even enjoyed the Laser Blast. Finally, it was dark when she had finished and yet she felt that a lot of things still remained to be seen and experienced. She told him, "We will come here again some other time."

He asked her, "Did you like it so much?"

"Oh, yes! It has been a wonderful day and I have enjoyed it to the hilt!" she replied, "Now, let us go back for I am extremely weary and sleepy."

While driving back, she slept for most of the time. When he asked her what she wanted to eat, she replied, "I just wish to sleep now. I have no energy left even to eat."

He stated, "But, I am hungry!"

She said, "Call for something in the room from the hotel or buy something on the way and have it in the hotel. I can't tell you how exhausted I feel."

He asked, "And what about the cheque?"

She questioned, "What about the cheque? Arrey, I did tell you it is yours. But I will give you tomorrow."

He repeated, "I don't desire the cheque for myself, but for

you. I can stay anywhere, but I am despising what you have to go through!"

She retaliated, "What do I have to go through? I am enjoying life. I can't understand your impatience for the cheque. Why have you suddenly become so anxious? You didn't even enjoy the day today. You were in a cocoon throughout."

He silenced her by imparting a kiss on her lips after stopping the car and then said, "Please bear with me. You will have to excuse me for any discomfort that I am causing you. I have been very particular to do the best for my wife and I can't tell you how I feel! Shit! I am a useless fellow – utterly useless! I have to beg with my wife for money when I should be providing her every possible comfort! I am the most useless man in the universe."

Suddenly, he began sobbing loudly. Very rarely had she seen a man cry and she was perplexed. She did not really know what to do. She also kissed him and said, "Darling! I understand your desire to give me the best and I think you are indeed giving me the best. I am very happy with you. And I shall be happy to be with you in whatever condition we are in. I did not marry you for your money. I married you because you liked me."

His eyes remained moist for long, even after they reached their room. Both of them did not eat anything that day. She took him in his arms, but was soon drowsy and drifted into the world of sleep, little knowing that next day would be the hardest night she would ever endure or would have heard of.

□

29

The Encashment

In the morning, Tanishk was again up before her. He kissed her to wake her up and said, "Darling! Haven't you slept a lot? You never get up this late and I was worried."

She lazily wrapped her arms around him and said, "Today, I want to get up late. Please let me sleep for another hour." She did not realise when she slept off again.

She was again woken up by a kiss. This time, she kissed him back. He began feeling her and she murmured, "You are in a cheeky mood today, aren't you?"

He didn't reply, but pulled her closer. They made love once again.

After freshening up, she remembered that he had been overanxious for the cheques the day before, and she opened her suitcase to find it. In the five days, she hardly had time to set her luggage properly and everything was in a mess. She could not find the cheques in the first glance and she began the hunt once again. He had been watching her every movement and uttered, "Have you lost the cheques? Why don't you keep things properly? You have become extremely lazy these days."

She giggled and said, "You males! You always find fault with your women! I am trying to locate it and you dare not call me lazy again. I am not used to so much of travelling. I am more of a loner and my world was limited to books." Then suddenly she remembered something and asked, "By the way, how did you know that I was looking for the cheques? I never mentioned!"

He also smiled and replied, "Darling! I did tell you what worries me in detail yesterday, didn't I? I want us to move into the apartment as soon as possible. And I am sorry if I hurt you – I didn't mean to say that you are actually lazy...it is just that everything is so bungled that..."

Seeing his nervousness, she decided to tease him even after she had found them. She kept telling him, "I can't find the cheques!"

His anger was clearly visible, though he did not say a word. Finally, he got up indignantly and was about to leave the room, when she stated with a grin on her face, "Come on, Tanishk! I am not as careless as you think me to be! I am a responsible person and I have become all the more sensible and mature after marriage. After all, I have been transformed into a woman from a girl and I do comprehend that marriage comes with responsibility. Here are the cheques..."

He embraced her and said, "I am so very lucky to have you dear! Sorry for my impatience...I didn't mean to behave the way I was...I don't know what overcame me! May be a sense of insecurity and vulnerability! Anyway, let us go and encash the cheques."

She stated, "I think you are forgetting! We have skipped dinner yesterday and I am damn hungry. Let us order something first."

Their hotel offered a wide range of Indian food on their menu and they ordered *dosa* in their room. Monika was a slow eater, while he was a fast one and as soon as he had finished, he said, "At least today, be fast! It is going to be a long day."

She stated, "Let me eat at my own pace. I can't eat food quickly. I enjoy every morsel of what passes through my gullet. After all, who knows whether I will get the next morsel?"

Gazing into her eyes, he said, "Since when have you become so philosophical?"

She replied, "I have always been like this. I have seen life take about turns so many times. When I have been happy for a moment, I have been ditched by destiny on the other. I have begun living in instants rather than periods. I try to get as much as possible from life till those moments exist."

His gaze into her eyes remained intense. He kissed her on her forehead gently and remained still with his eyes closed. She felt as if it was the most loveable moments of their married life. After some time, he said, "Come, let us go now. You do wish to see the De Louvre in detail, don't you? I have seen your interest in these kinds of things and I am sure that you will take at least three days to finish your complete tour of De Louvre. Let us begin today. May be, you can go alone subsequently."

She asked, "Go alone? But why? Why, won't you accompany me?"

He replied, "Arrey? I will start working *naa*? When will I have time after that?"

She said, "We can come on weekends, can't we?"

He looked at her contemplatively and replied, "Yes, we can!" She wondered why his voice lacked lustre and enthusiasm.

She put on a denim and a tee and was about to wear her sandals rather than shoes, but he said, "Please, put on the shoes. It can be annoyingly cool. The weather does not seem good." He also made her wear a leather jacket, which he helped her put on. He kissed her – his kiss was neither passionate, nor wild. It smelt of love. Just before they were leaving, he said, "While encashing the travellers' cheques, if the persons ask you why you are doing it, it is better to say that you are transferring the money in a bank account rather than saying that it is for apartment renovation."

"But why? And why will they ask me? After all, it is my money and I will do whatever I wish," she stated.

He said, "The Europeans ask too many questions if it is related to an apartment. For now, just listen to me. I will answer all your questions subsequently."

They began with their itinerary for the day with the encashing of the cheques. The lady sitting on the counter did ask her the reason for taking out such a huge amount and she convinced her. Tanishk seemed to be extremely joyful after that. She loved his exuberant mood and joined him in the fun.

There was so much to see in De Louvre and they were already a bit late. She began her tour with the paintings section and went to see Mona Lisa. She had read so much about the painting and had been fascinated by it. The galleria was full of lovely paintings and she spent more than two hours over there and still felt unsatisfied. They had a look at the other paintings before they reached the place where Picasso's paintings were available. She was simply zapped.

Afterwards, they had their lunch and then proceeded to the sculpture section and kept moving from hall to hall, till she was extremely tired. She said, "I haven't had enough, but we will have to come here some other day. Promise me that you will bring me."

He hesitated. She asked angrily, "Why do you dither so much? You just said in the morning that you will get me here on weekends!"

He said, "I am not dithering! We will come for sure!"

She did not even have the courage to walk to the parking space and she asked him to bring the car to the exit. After she had sat down, he said, "I will take you to a wonderful restaurant today. It has a live Indian orchestra and I am sure that you will love it."

She replied, "All I want to do is to go back to the hotel and have a nice nap."

He said, "Hey, Monika! Listen to me and let us go there for once. I am sure you will love the place as well as the food. And then, it is a special day for me. It is my birthday today."

She looked at him open-mouthed, "What? It is your birthday and you didn't tell me? So bad of you!"

He chuckled, "Did you ask me?"

She said, "We were so lost that we forgot all this. Let us go and celebrate."

After they had driven for a few miles, suddenly the car stopped. He got down to investigate, but the car simply refused to start, no matter how much ever he tried. She asked, "What do we do now?"

He replied, "Why worry? Car is not the only mode of transport in Paris! We have very good taxis and then...there is the Metro train. Have you ever travelled by Metro?"

She replied, "I had heard of Metro in Delhi and Kolkata back in India, but never really used it. I thought it was rather fascinating, but have always been afraid of mobs."

He grinned, "You won't find such a mob in Paris. The people are rather well-behaved. You will see for yourself as we board one. Let me call the mechanic first so that he can take care of the car and get it for us at the hotel."

They soon approached the nearest Metro station. It was a rather confusing name and she could not pronounce it. She was lost in seeing the environment around when he asked her to board a Metro which had already arrived, without a sound.

□

30
The Treachery

Monika found the system of Metro quite fascinating. He explained to her the pertinent points which were to be taken care of while travelling in a Metro. By that time, they had reached another Metro station and he asked her to get down. “We have to change the train,” he informed.

When they embarked, she was stunned to see the vastness of the station. He informed her that it was the terminal that connected several lines and added, “I always get lost in this station and find it difficult to find my way. Let me just be sure of where to go and I will be back. Till that time, you just sit here.”

She said, “No! I won’t sit alone! I am afraid of the vastness of the place. Let me come with you.”

He stated, “You are very adamant, aren’t you? Things will be done faster if I go and find out since I may have to walk a lot. You are already tired. You should listen to me sometimes, for your own sake.”

Although she was not happy with his suggestion, she sat on a seat boorishly. She looked at the clock just over her head. It was 8 o’clock. She calculated in her mind, ‘I suppose, it will be 8.30 by the time we reach our destination and then we will take at least an hour for dinner. I assume it will be 10.30 or 11 p.m. by the time we reach the hotel.’

She looked around. A group of young girls was standing in a circle. Most of them wore minis with stockings and a jacket. She wondered how they could remain so scantily dressed in the biting cold. Despite a leather jacket, she could feel the numbness in her body. And the exposed portions of the body, such as the palms and nose, were almost frozen.

She looked at her watch. It was 8.15 p.m. and he had not yet returned. She continuously stared at the clock as its minute hand moved from 3 to 12, which meant that it was an hour since he had left. She was worried by now. The anger had been substituted by anxiety and various thoughts started floating in her mind. Had he been hurt? Had he met with an accident? She looked in her purse for her mobile to connect to him. It was missing!

She panicked. Even in the freezing cold, she began to sweat profusely. She was all alone in a foreign land about which she hardly knew! She thought of moving towards the entrance. But the entrance was so colossal that she was frightened once again and she returned back to the same spot where she had been sitting. May be, Tanishk may appear all of a sudden!

For her, time had come to a standstill; but the needles of the clock kept moving. The mob was thinning out and finally, there were hardly any persons on the platform. She looked at the clock. It was 11 p.m. She had an intuition that someone was staring at her. She was rattled and she ran towards the entrance at full speed. She saw the ticket-checkers at the end of the corridor. She remembered that the tickets were with Tanishk. What if they caught her? Hurriedly she took a turn. The turn led to a staircase which further headed towards another platform. How many platforms did the damned station have? She returned back, but she was completely lost. In her hurry, she dashed against a man who fell down by the sheer virtue of the suddenness. She gave him a hand for him to get up and apologised, "I…I am very sorry…I…"

He was an Indian and said in Hindi, "*Bahen, dekhkar chala karo.*" (Sister, you should watch while you walk.) However, seeing her terrified face, he asked her, "What is the matter?"

Seeing the sympathy in his words, she broke down and explained to him everything. However, by the end of the story, his sympathy had changed into arrogance and he stated, "You all are scoundrels. The lure of a foreign country makes you come here by hook or by crook and then, you begin narrating such stories to gain sympathy!" Catching her hand, he said loudly, "I am going to hand you over to the police."

She suddenly remembered that she did not even have her passport with her! She used full force and kicked him on his groin. While he was trying to stabilise himself, she ran and hid herself in the ladies washroom. She remained inside one of the cubicles for almost half an hour and then she came out noiselessly. The man was no longer there. She thanked God. She kept moving from one place to other in search of an exit and when she found one, she felt as if she had come out of a gas chamber.

She felt better once she was outside. She did remember the name of the hotel where they stayed, but was not able to recollect the area. She asked a passerby how far it was. Thankfully, the way was quite straight, though it was at a distance of about an hour's walk. The man asked her to take a taxi. She searched in her purse. She just had five Euros and a few cents. She could not get a taxi and she walked down.

It was past midnight when she finally reached the hotel. Though she was extremely exhausted, she was extremely happy to find that a familiar receptionist was there at the desk. The lady was a Chinese named Mei and they had often exchanged pleasantries. Seeing her, she said, "Hello ma'am! How can I help you?"

Monika replied, "Did my husband reach here?"

She stated, "Oh, yes! He did! And he vacated the room long back."

She could not believe what she had heard. Tanishk had come and vacated the room? Surely, there was some misunderstanding. Or maybe, Mei had heard something wrong. She repeated, "Mei, I am asking about my husband – Tanishk!"

She questioned, "Tanishk? That must be a pet name I suppose. He was Animesh, wasn't he?"

Monika asked, "What?" She felt that the whole world was revolving. She enquired again, "Do you remember me correctly? I am the person who used to stay in room number..."

She replied, "Of course, I do! How can I forget such a beautiful lady? In fact, I was a bit worried when he came all alone to vacate the room. Is there an issue dear?"

She hesitated. She had told everything to that stranger on the station and had seen his reaction. What if Mei were to react the same way? But did she have any other option?

Monika narrated to Mei her entire tale. Finally, she was again amidst tears. Mei held her hand and said, "Monika, I am very sorry to hear all this. Let me show you the copy of the bill that was paid by him." The bill was indeed in the name of Animesh Kapoor! She was absolutely shocked! She had been fooled from the beginning by him! She felt dizzy, but was supported by Mei and the other hotel staff. Mei got her some cold drink and fruits to eat and asked, "Let me know what I can do to help you. I hope you have your passport and other documents with you. We could report to the police..."

Monika replied with tears in her eyes, "I don't have anything with me."

Mei said, "Okay, I will open a room for you for the night. Take some sleep and then decide what should be the future course of action. Maybe, you should call up your guardians from your country."

Though she lay on the bed, sleep was elusive. She had been stung by the poison of treachery by someone posing as her husband. As she recollected the moments of love, she wondered how he could act so well. When she was with him, what she had thought to be normal seemed a practiced fraud. All the while, he had been waiting to lay his hands upon her money and the moment he had that, he had left her alone to fend for herself!

Monika's mind understood very well that she had been betrayed. However, her heart still refused to accept. She made her plans for the next day. After all, he had shown her his house as well his workplace. She decided to go to his office and tell his boss about the treason and demand justice. If not, she could go to his apartment and question him.

Finally, early in the morning, when it was time to wake up, her exhausted eyes closed and she drifted into the world of sleep. Though it was a disturbed sleep and she kept murmuring something or the other, she did sleep for a few hours.

□

31

The Search

Monika got up with a knock at the door. Mei came inside and said, "Monika, I can understand your distress; but it is time for you to vacate the room. I had allowed you to sleep on my own account. The hotel rules do not allow us."

Getting up, she told her, "I am and shall remain utterly grateful to you for all that you have done for me. But, how are you here now? Isn't your shift over?"

She replied, "Yes, it was over long back. I was worried for you and decided to wait." Handing her a visiting card, she continued, "These are my contact details. Do let me know if I can be of any help." She hugged her and then went away.

By now, Monika was sure that Tanishk had indeed vanished into thin air, taking away everything – the money, the jewellery and even the trust! His name was also false. She wondered how on earth she ended up trusting such a fraudster! Anyway, she decided to confront him and take him to the court, if required. After all, she knew where he stayed and where he worked.

She decided to begin with her search at his apartment. They had visited it during their hop-on hop-off bus tour. She tried hard to recollect where the spot was. She had been so safe in the presence of Tanishk that she had never thought it necessary to notice. However, she did remember the Opera and the ice-cream parlour. She asked the receptionist how she could reach Opera. It was almost half an hour's walk and since she did not have cash, she decided to use her feet only. She soon located the ice-cream parlour too, and from there, it was not tough for her to reach the apartment which Tanishk had said belonged to him.

There was no one at the entrance and the door was locked. She remembered that Tanishk had stated that in this part of the world, everything was electronically controlled. She waited for someone to appear. After a few minutes, when she saw a man coming out, she was jubilant. He appeared to be an old man. He was bald and walked with a stoop. As soon as he came out of the gate, she said, "Uncle, I need your help..."

He immediately answered, "I don't help saleswomen," and went off without giving her a chance to speak. She was a bit sad, but she decided not to give up. After all, it was a question of life and death. She decided to wait. Almost an hour passed with no one either going out or coming in. Finally, she saw a woman coming towards the gate and she told her story, requesting her to take her to Tanishk's apartment. She even told her the name of Animesh, in case he was known by that name. The woman was a stout, short and black woman. She stared at her from head to toe and then arrogantly replied, "There is no one by the name of Tanishk or Animesh here." She tried to explain the issue she was facing, but the woman refused to listen. And yet, she decided not to give up.

She saw a teenager coming out jovially with earplugs on her ears. For a moment she thought that it was no use talking to her, but then she remembered that no opportunity should be lost. And when she did, she was happy she had not let go. The girl, Lara, was kind indeed. Asking her to wait, she said, "I will get my Mom. Please wait here."

When she returned, she was with the black woman once again. She wondered at the contrast. The girl was fair and looked entirely different. The woman had refused to listen to her when she had requested, but her daughter seemed to have convinced her and she was ready to listen to her distress. When she heard the complete story, she said with finality in her tone, "The guy has fooled you dear. No Indian lives in this apartment, nor have I seen anyone since the last two years."

She asked her about the Sri Lankan lady and the Pakistani guy whom her husband had mentioned. There indeed was a Sri Lankan lady, and the dark lady summoned her downstairs. She also did not know any Tanishk or Animesh!

For Monika, this was but an affirmation of the fact that a well-planned treachery had been played upon her. Still, she did not wish to leave the final straw and decided to check at Deere International, his office. They had crossed his office on way to Versailles, but she was not sure where exactly it was. Then she thought, 'It was such a big office; I am sure people know it.' She saw a policeman standing at a square and asked him for the directions. She understood that the place was far enough for her to go by foot. He informed her about the bus which would take her there. She thanked him and walked towards the bus-stop, wondering all the while how much money it would take for her to reach there. She asked someone standing on the bus-stop about the fare and she grasped with difficulty the fact that with the money she had, she could only go there and not come back. She had already left herself to fate and decided to go.

Once she reached the office, she looked at its vastness and pondered if she could trace him in this big office. Nevertheless, she approached the security personnel at the gate and told them her story. They listened sympathetically and then one of them took her to the liaison officer's chamber.

The liaison officer, Anne Strong, was briefed by the security person about her in brief. She seemed to be a rather sweet lady. She asked her, "Do you have any of his photographs?"

Suddenly, Monika remembered his reluctance right from the beginning to get photographed. But she did have one of his photos in her handbag which was given to her by Susy, the journalist. She handed it to Anne, who looked at the photograph with interest and then began scanning her computer. Finally, she concluded, "No dear! No such guy works here!"

Monika was shocked. What sort of a check had his uncle exercised on the guy called Tanishk before marrying her to him? His name was false, his place of stay was incorrect and now, even his place of work was fabricated!

Monika felt dizzy once again. She tried to control herself, but couldn't and fell down. Anne supported her and took her to the infirmary. She was given glucose water and she felt better. Anne asked her to lie down for some time and also got her some sandwiches to eat. While she was gulping the sandwiches, she remembered that she had not eaten anything!

After she had stabilised a little, she was shocked by what Anne informed her. She said, "Monika, you seem to be a very innocent and naïve girl; but this man is a crook. This is the second time I have seen this photograph. I remember it very vividly, because the girl who had come to us with this photograph was also a very beautiful and well-educated Indian girl. I wonder how he fooled you too."

Was there any doubt that she was indeed stupid? Right since her parent's death, everyone had been fooling her and taking her for granted. Her wish and desire was not at all honoured even for her own marriage. There was hurry in everything as if she was a burden on *chacha* and *chachi*. She could still understand *chachi*, but surely not *chacha*. Right from the time of her marriage, he had seemed too distant. Why, he hadn't even called her to ask if she was alright after she landed in Paris.

And then, her thoughts once again diverted towards Tanishk. What a well-planned conspiracy it was! He acted as if he was in love with her. Despite his knowledge of the fact that she loved Gurpreet, he kept pursuing her. He did not leave her even after her attempted suicide. During their marriage also, there were no relatives from his side – just a few drunken hooligans. She wondered if they really were his relatives. She remembered her attempts at asking him to introduce his parents, but which were continuously thwarted by him saying that his mother was admitted in hospital. Was she really admitted? Or were his parents also on hire when they had come to see her?

She herself had not been able to see his deceit because she was submerged in her own grief of having to lose Gurpreet, but she wondered why her *chacha* had not thought of it! How had he accepted the non-availability of the groom's parents during marriage? Had Tanishk been too shrewd to convince them with his sweet talk or was *chacha* also involved in some way?

Anne asked her, "Is there anything else I can do for you, Monika?"

Monika remembered that she did not have any money and she did wish to connect to *chacha* to check his stand – whether he really loved her and had done everything for her sake or was he also involved in Tanishk's conspiracy!

She said hesitantly, "If I could make a phone call to India, it would be great."

□

32

Settling Down

Monika was so lost in the past that she had completely forgotten where she was and whom she was talking to. Shekhar's voice brought her back from her reverie. He asked Monika, "And your *chacha* refused to help, isn't it?"

Till then, Shekhar had only been listening; he hadn't uttered a word. But this simple sentence meant that he was in complete synchrony with her and comprehended what she felt and what her condition was. He could also guess that her *chacha* must have refused help to her.

She replied, "Yes. He was more worried about the loss of money rather than my awful situation here. He did offer to buy flight tickets for me, but was apprehensive that I may try to take back the reigns of my father's business."

He questioned, "Why don't you? I suppose it will be the best. You should return back to India and ask him to hand over everything to you. After all, that is what your father always desired till he was alive. The business belongs to you. You are neither homeless nor penniless. From what Roopam told me, you are worth millions."

She stated, "Shekhar, I had thought about it even when I was in India. My father did desire my taking over his business empire. However, I am a witness to something that occurred towards the end of his life. Though he never specified, but he was going through some trouble which took away not only his life, but also killed my mother and brother and jeopardised my life. Thinking of that makes me numb. I do not wish to take over the business. Neither was he fit for business, nor am I. A gentle person can't handle any business."

He asked, "Then what do you plan to do now? Have you thought of anything? Do you wish to go back to India or do you plan to stay over?"

She stated, "I think I would love to stay back. However, since I do not have a passport, I don't think I can...I mean I do not know the rules and was afraid of coming across any police official."

He explained, "Since you have been provided with visa for temporary stay, you are registered and we can report the loss of your passport and get it reissued; though the entire process is long drawn and shall take time. We have to first decide what you wish to do."

She hesitated, "I am penniless and that is a cause of concern in whatever decision I wish to take."

He said, "First, be sure of what you wish to do. If you do desire something sincerely and seriously, the paths get lighted on their own."

She stated, after a pause, "After the recent incidents that have taken place in my life, I do not wish to go back to India. I think I wish to study literature here, if possible. I am a post-graduate in English literature and would love to continue with it."

He said, "Let me work in the direction. I will find out the rules and regulations and also discuss with someone in the university. However, I think we have a problem here. You will have to learn French, since that is the media of communication in most of the universities here."

She replied, "I know it quite well. I had learnt it to impress Tanishk."

He added, "I will have to first struggle to get your duplicate mark-sheets, but I suppose Resham will help us with that. Have belief in your own self and things will be set right by and by."

She stated, "More than me, I believe in you and Roopam. Had you both not been here, I would be begging on the streets. I don't know if I shall ever be able to repay you."

He said, "You are like a sister to me whom I had lost in early childhood. Sisters don't repay. They ask."

Life soon began moving smoothly for Monika. Though it was not at all the way she had imagined, but then, certain things happen in life the way they are meant to be. Neither more, nor less. She only took everything as a lesson in life. Of course, a police complaint was dutifully lodged, but she expected nothing out of it. May be, that was what moving on in life meant.

Earlier Shekhar and Roopam had suggested that they would loan her the money required for her studies, but that was not required. It is said that luck favours the brave and she was indeed fortunate to have received a scholarship for her studies. Monika stayed for a few months with Shekhar and Roopam, but soon moved on to a hostel after she received her scholarship. She loved them a lot, but she wanted the relationship to stay as it was. Sometimes, too much of closeness destroys a relationship.

She continued visiting Shekhar and Roopam. They were the only ones she had in the world, besides Resham. She visited them on weekends without fail and she loved being there. They would often shop together and also have quite a few rendezvous together.

One weekend, Shekhar was not home and Roopam and Monika decided to go out to eat. While they were waiting for their order to come, Roopam asked her, "Don't you remember Gurpreet? Resham was telling that he is not married yet. He wishes to talk to you. She asked me to connect both of you."

Monika questioned, "Did you ever talk to Gurpreet since you came to Paris?"

Resham was pensive and she replied after a while, "Monika, the two situations are different. Gurpreet was my first love, but he never loved me as I explained to you earlier. I am completely satisfied with my life. Shekhar is the best man I could have had. I do not wish to belittle my love for Shekhar in any manner. I have moved on. But neither of you have moved on, have you? Somewhere deep in your heart, he still has a permanent seat. And he also did not get married which indicates that he still loves you. He is waiting for you and I feel that you should connect with him."

She replied, "I think, I have also moved on. Gurpreet no longer interests me."

However, her mind kept wandering after that. She so much wished him to hold her tight in his embrace. And then she remembered, had he really loved her, he would never have let her go. She was never charmed by the projected wealth of Tanishk nor was she lured by the prospect of going abroad. She had only desired Gurpreet and his love. He had rejected her love and left her to be with Tanishk, who had cheated her and left her alone forever. Never could she again believe in love. There indeed was nothing called true love; people faked love for different reasons. Tanishk had faked love for money. *Chacha* had faked love for control of her business. The only thing she could not understand was why Gurpreet had faked love. She let the question remain. Time would reveal on its own. And then, certain questions are better left unanswered for the replies often make one feel empty. Emptiness was already a part of her life and she did not wish to let it multiply further.

When the negativity of thoughts would surround Monika or when the pain would be too much to bear, she would dip herself into books. She loved the world of fiction. It would take her into an imaginary place with the characters of the book would play their roles in front of her, while she remained a silent spectator. She could neither choose the course their lives would follow, nor could she judge them. They just passed in front of her eyes, each of them sharing their secrets with her. Some of them were the romantic secrets, some were the secrets of life and some were plain mysteries, but each character made her wiser.

One day, when the thoughts were too disturbing, she picked up a pen and paper and began pouring her feelings on them in the form of poetry. Her thoughts flowed uninterruptedly and she loved what she had written. After that, the thoughts no longer disturbed her and she got a sound sleep. Did writing have a psychopathic healing effect, she wondered?

And then it became her routine. After returning home, she would spend most of the time in reading, but after that she would write something, mostly in the form of poetry. Her diary became her closest pal. Of course, there were phone calls from Resham and these made her feel really loved. They talked at least once in a week and discussed almost everything. However, there was a subject which Resham never touched, though she wished to do so desperately. She had promised Gurpreet that she won't ever talk about him to Monika and she respected her promise.

□

33
Love Happens...

Monika's life passed peacefully. It had been almost two years since the time she had got married and left her motherland, but she did not really miss it. After all, there was nothing really worth missing. True, she missed the house she was brought up in; but that just a materialistic thing. She missed the city of Patiala, but she enjoyed the city of Paris. May be, to gain something, you have to lose something.

The new country had welcomed her with open arms. She even had a few friends by then. Kate, who was also involved in research in the same university, though in History and her boyfriend, Steve were pretty close and she spent a few evenings with the two of them. And then there was Paul, who had turned into a friend besides being her guide. Paul was just a few years elder to her and the love for literature had brought them close to each other. When she told him about the richness of Indian literature, he even began learning a little of Hindi. When she would sit and sip a cup of coffee with her new friends, she would often remember the saying that when one end of the thread breaks, there is another thread which joins it. The strength of coupling determines the endurance of the bond.

Another thing that she learnt the hard way was that often it is not blood relations who really help in life; sometimes, it is the friends who form a much more solid connect. After her parents' death, Resham and her family were the ones who had provided her the strength to face all the hardships she had faced. Roopam had provided her support despite the early misunderstanding that they had in life. Her husband, Shekhar, treated her like a sister and she was so happy to have him as a brother. And her friends at the university were making her survive gleefully, especially, Paul! She often wondered how a person from a different nationality and an entirely different upbringing could become so close, while her own relatives had grown so far apart that she no longer remembered them.

Monika often wondered which culture was better – the Indian culture where relationships were considered very strong or the Western culture which was much freer. However, she could not find an answer. In her early childhood, she had often heard that the Western culture did not respect traditions and was valueless which was resulting in degrading morals. She pondered what were the moral values learnt by her *chacha* or Tanishk!

Despite registering the case, no trace had been made in locating Tanishk. She had been interrogated quite often and she had tried to give every detail as best as she could remember, but she was not a good observer. Had she been one, she would not have let herself be fooled so easily.

One day, while discussing with Paul, she had vented out all her sealed anger against destiny and told her everything about Tanishk. She had asked him, "Tell me Paul, what is my status? Am I married or unmarried? And if I am married, how do I take a divorce against my husband who can't be located by the best of police forces?"

Paul could not find any answer to her query. He only tried to comfort her by saying that time itself finds an answer to many questions. What else could he say? He still could not understand so many customs which Monika had explained to him as tradition. Had there not been the social evil called dowry, may be, Monika's fate would have been different. But then, he would never have got to know Monika and would have missed an important chapter of his life.

Paul had felt intrigued by Monika and her dedication right from the time she had come to him for her thesis. Those pair of eyes seemed to hold huge history in them, which he could never guess. They somehow always reminded him of Mitchell, his first and only love.

Mitchell was a cartoonist, a rather blunt and outspoken person. And he simply loved her for her straightforwardness and adored her for her courage. The time when he had met her would always stay alive in front of his eyes.

Paul was waiting at the station for his train to arrive. He had reached rather early in view of the excitement of meeting his mother. He decided to roam outside to kill time, when he came across an exhibition of cartoons. An admirer of all forms of art, he got engrossed in seeing them and decided to ask the cartoonist if the cartoons were on sale. Purchasing something from an artist was a token of appreciation.

What Paul had expected was that the cartoonist would be a grownup, mature lady, but when he saw a young blonde with a pony tail, he couldn't believe that it was indeed her. He asked her twice if indeed she was the cartoonist and she laughed, "Why? Can't you believe that I can draw? Let me draw you and you will see for yourself."

Taking out a pencil and a paper, she drew him in two minutes. The only feature she had modified to make the cartoon was his nose, which she had lengthened to make it appear a right-angled triangle. On it was placed a big mole.

He laughed at it and said, "You are indeed marvellous and one of your kind..."

"Mitchell...my name is Mitchell...," she said.

He raised his hand for a shake and said, "Paul. Let us be friends, Mitchell. I really admire your talent and believe me, I wasn't making fun of you."

He bought the cartoon and left to meet his mother wondering if they would ever meet again. He wondered if it was 'love at first sight' for him all through the way. Even his mother teased him if there was a girl in his life.

Their meeting would have remained a simple encounter had it not been for another cartoon which appeared in a newspaper which had her familiar signature. He rushed to the newspaper's office to get her contact details. The officer was unwilling to part with her details till he told him that he loved the girl.

Since then, they remained a couple. She shifted to his residence and they stayed together for six months when she surprised him by informing that she was pregnant. He proposed to her for a marriage and everything looked like a fairytale until...

The memories of the day were itched in his mind. Mitchell had begun working permanently with a newspaper by then. She had drawn a powerful cartoon a week ago which was a wit on God when millions of people were hungry in the world. She had won quite a few accolades for it. Both of them had decided to celebrate the success with their common friends and had hosted a party for them. Paul dropped her at the gate of the restaurant and went to park his car. When he returned, he saw that she was surrounded by two men in black attire, pointing a gun at her forehead. He was stunned; he screamed, "Leave her alone."

Without looking at him, the man shouted, "This is for all those who dare to defame our God" and two bullets were fired at her point blank. The men disappeared as quickly as they had appeared, leaving him devastated for life. Mitchell was rushed to the hospital, but she could not survive. The entire world had stood up in support of her, but that certainly could not bring back his Mitchell.

There was an acute resemblance between Monika and Mitchell though they were from two different countries. The only things that were not similar were the colour of the hair and the gentleness in Monika. Right from the time Monika had entered his room, she had reminded him of Mitchell and he had accepted her as his student for thesis. Her knowledge and her command over literature surprised him.

But there was a wall between the two of them. Monika had been ditched and she had stopped believing in love. Paul could never really come out of the memories of Mitchell.

Finally, after almost a year, Paul decided to break the wall and invited her for a cup of coffee at the Coffee House. This was an invitation which surprised Monika. However, she agreed. After all, she liked him. On their very first personal meeting, he told her all about Mitchell. Bound by the loss of their love, they became very good friends. The bond kept getting stronger every passing day and finally, they came so close that they began spending almost every evening together.

When Paul's mother came to meet him, he introduced her to Monika and both of them seemed to gel very well. This pleased him a lot. After Mitchell, they were the only two persons he loved.

□

34

Departure

Another year passed. Monika's thesis was submitted and her studies were coming to an end. She was one of the youngest scholars to have submitted her thesis, that too in such a short time. Paul had been very much impressed by her work and to ensure that it deserved the attention he was giving it, he even invited one of his own senior professors to read it. He was happy to note that she passed all tests with flying colours.

Paul was very much drawn towards Monika, but he lacked the courage to propose. However, he did understand that after Monika left the university, he may miss her. He had already missed Mitchell and he did not wish to let slip Monika from his life. The dilemma of whether he should reveal his love for her was giving him sleepless nights. His beard had grown long and his hair was unkempt. His eyes were red due to lack of sleep, they bulged out. One evening she teased him, "Either you are drunk these days or you are in love with someone."

He kept staring at her, still not sure if he should say or not.

Kate and Steve had also been observing that something was wrong with Paul and they decided to discuss the matter with him one evening when Monika had gone to meet Shekhar and Roopam. Kate asked him, "Why don't you reveal what is in your heart to Monika?"

He was astonished to comprehend that they had understood his love for Monika and kept fidgeting. Steve patted his back and said, “It is quite obvious that you both are in love with each other. Better say it.”

He questioned, “What if she doesn’t? What if that destroys even the friendship?”

Steve explained, “One has to take a calculated risk. As such, Monika shall be leaving us soon. May be, you can halt her departure. And then, you have nothing to lose. If anything, there will be a gain.”

However, what was so obvious to both of them as well as to the whole world was unknown to Monika. Since she had stopped believing in love, she felt that the entire world also had stopped loving. She thought that the bond that she and Paul shared was simple and plain friendship. Thus, she found it very strange when Paul invited her for dinner in a very special way by sending her an invitation with a rose. She obviously agreed to go, for she had never denied any of his invitations.

When she reached Le Meurice, the place that he had invited her, she was amazed to see the grandeur of the place and walked open-eyed. She wondered if she had even worn a dress suitable for the occasion. Paul normally preferred street food and was not much interested in the lavishness and luxury of the place. This change of stance astonished her.

Right at the moment she entered, the orchestra began playing lovely music. She looked around to see if they were singing for someone else, but when she found that she was the object of their attention, she was coy and walked gently to the place where Paul was sitting. The main singer of the orchestra asked them both to join for a dance. She had just learned salsa and she tapped her foot on music. She was on cloud nine. Never had she felt so cherished.

After they had danced for nearly an hour, he bent on his knees in front of everyone present in the dining hall and presenting her another rose, said, “Monika, I take pride in saying that I love you. Do you love me too?”

Monika looked around. The orchestra had begun playing a romantic number. All around, everyone was looking at her, expecting her to say 'yes'. She also didn't wish to hurt Paul. She wondered how he would feel if she said 'no' for she knew how sensitive he was. However, she had no option. 'Love' was a feeling she had divorced long ago. She just could not understand it any longer and was strongly averse to it. Otherwise, who could refuse an adorable person such as Paul? She knew that if she agreed, he would treat her in a manner that she had only read in novels. But, that would be an injustice. She was frozen as ice and his love was not enough to melt her; or, may be, its warmth had not reached her. Or, was it that she still loved Gurpreet? His face flashed again in front of her eyes and she stiffened. Why did her thoughts jump again and again to him?

Impulsively, she took an about turn and ran from there as fast as she could. Though there were many taxis available, she didn't take any of them. She kept running and running as much as she could. She did not even halt at the squares with red signals. A long line of vehicles would come to a screeching halt at the squares she passed through. Finally, when she reached Pantheon, she realised how long she had run. She sat on its step in disdain. Lowering her head on her lap, she began to weep loudly.

After she had cried to her heart's content, she took a taxi and reached her hostel. At the entry, she saw Paul waiting for her. His hat was in his hand despite the chilly weather. He stood leaning against the pillar. Seeing him, she wondered since when he had been standing like that. She was sad to have hurt him. Hugging him tight, she said, "Paul...Paul...I would have really liked to say that I do love you, but I can't Paul...I do adore you, but in a different way...certainly not romantically...I am sorry...really sorry..."

Giving her a peck on her cheek, he said, "Monika, I understand...I completely understand you dear. I only thought that just in case you do love me, it should be the best of your days...I simply wished to give you all the love that you had missed all your life...nothing much...I honour your decision dear and wish the very best for you...but why did you run away like that? You could have simply refused me..."

Putting her little finger on his lips, she stated, "I didn't wish to hurt you. I know what you have gone through. But..."

He said, "I know, Monika. You either love a person or you don't. I apologise to you for being so candid."

Time stood still for both of them. They were locked in an embrace for quite some time after which he said, "In case you have forgiven my silliness, can we be friends? Can we go out to dine?"

They went to a small restaurant near her hostel where they had simple food. The ice was soon broken and it was just like old days. They laughed and talked till it was time for the restaurant to close down.

Though everything seemed to be like old days, Monika observed that Paul seemed to have suddenly aged after that. The frequency of their meetings decreased. There was a thread in him which looked broken, though he never mentioned it.

One day, he called her out for a dinner once again. He looked very lean and thin that day. He informed her, "Monika, you will be glad to know that the university has accepted you as a temporary faculty."

She was quite surprised since she had never applied for a post. She said, "Oh Paul! You are such a sweetheart! I know that you have done this for me. But there was no vacancy, I feel?"

He replied, "There is going to be one soon. Monika, I had called you since I wished that you should be the first one to know. I have resigned from my post. I have taken up the services of the church and shall devote myself completely to His work. I am leaving next week. I nominated you and this was gladly accepted by everyone."

She stared at him blankly. For quite some time she did not know what to say. She should have been happy to get an appointment at the university; but she just couldn't be. After all, it had come at a cost. The price was the departure of her best friend. She also knew the reason why he was leaving and felt guilty. She had always thought that she would be the one to go, but destiny had something else in store for them, which was revealed only now.

A week passed in a jiffy. The two of them stayed almost together for most of the time. Paul gave her everything before going and these included his apartment, though she kept refusing. He said, "If I come to visit this city, I will be happy to see my house that once was with a dear friend." Only his clothes were distributed to the poor.

Finally, it was time for him to leave. As she hugged him at the airport, she knew that a slice of her was bidding adieu. Strange is life! Paul had taught her to love without expecting; a lesson she was to remember for life. Even while going, he had only given her something.

□

35
A Call from India

Monika's life moved at a slow pace after that. Till then, Paul had been there to share the moments. With him gone, there was a strange and eerie silence. It was almost as if winter had covered her and it was snowing all around while she stood frozen in it. The sun of happiness was no longer visible. There was murkiness all around. Stillness was evident in all moments. During daytime, she went to the university and it was fine. Her evenings and nights were mostly spent in taciturnity. The television irritated her. Going out did not interest her any longer. Negative thoughts would often surround her, invading her mind from all directions. The question, 'why this had to happen with me?' pestered her more and more.

Initially, she did not pay much attention to it. However, one day she fell down in the university and was taken to the hospital by her colleagues and from that time onwards, she became more careful. She began spending her time in writing and reading. These hobbies took her in a world away from her own world and negative thoughts found it difficult to enter her mind.

Her friends, Kate and Steve sealed their love with marriage. She wondered about the differences in her own motherland and the country she was in, once again. Here, people married for love. There was no money involved, though there had been many cases of demand for huge alimony in divorce. They obviously did not have the parental approval for selecting their guy or girl, but the parents did accept the choice of their children happily. The divorce rate was surely higher, and she wondered what was better – suffering since one couldn't remarry or divorcing?

Mostly Kate and Steve included her in their weekend sojourns and she never felt unwanted in their company. Rather, she looked forward for them. The only thing which irritated her was their unsuccessful trials to link her with someone or the other. They just could not believe that she was not interested in the other sex.

One day, Shekhar called her to inform that Roopam was in family way and was unwell. She had become really fond of the couple and rushed to their house. Since Roopam was advised bed rest, she shifted temporarily to their house to take care of her. Though she knew that it was the only option available, but initially she felt a bit irritated at her change of routine. However, slowly she began enjoying the long discussions she would have with Roopam, as well as Shekhar. When she had shifted with them initially, she had been so immersed in her own grief that she could not see beyond. Since Roopam knew her from her childhood, she felt free to discuss everything with her. Shekhar was another lovable person and he was always welcome in their discussions.

Shekhar had completed his tenure and was transferred to Belgium. Since they were in the middle of a tough period, Roopam decided to stay back in Paris till she was better, while Shekhar went to join his new assignment. One day, while they were chatting, there was a call from India that surprised her and yet made her very happy. Resham was getting married!

Resham had begun teaching in a school at Patiala after she had completed her studies. Initially, she took Shantanu to be the father of her student Aarti, since he would come for all her parent-teacher meetings, though she often felt that he was a bit young to be her father.

Aarti was a rather mischievous student, always harassing someone or the other. The only person she would listen to without any queries would be Resham and everyone would bring all her complaints to her.

That particular day, Resham was extremely tired and was resting in the staff room with her head down, when another teacher brought Aarti to her and said, "I have asked the principal ma'am to rusticate this child from school. She has beaten Nayna black and blue and had to be hospitalised. She is crossing all limits."

Resham, already enervated, asked Aarti to stand in a corner holding her ears and said, "From now on, I am not going to talk to you."

At that moment, Resham was summoned by the principal and after that she had four continuous periods. When she returned, she found Aarti still standing in the same position. Seeing Resham, she simply said, "I will do anything you wish me to do, but please don't stop talking to me," and collapsed.

Resham had not really expected her to stand for so long. Perplexed, she immediately rushed her to a doctor and asked another teacher to give a call to her parents. At the hospital, Shantanu also joined her soon and together they tended to Aarti. The doctor said that Aarti had had received some shock.

Finally, when Aarti stabilised a little, Resham bid her goodbye. Shantanu came to leave her outside and said, "Ma'am, I can't find words to thank you for taking care of Aarti."

Resham had been surprised that the girl's mother had not yet arrived and she said, "Why don't you call her mother? I think she requires female company..."

Shantanu replied, "Ma'am, Aarti is my niece. My sister is dead. Her husband remarried and since Aarti could not digest the news, I brought her with me. I think that explains her slightly erratic behaviour, which, though is not justifiable, but....actually, my sister used to look a lot like you and that is why she regards you with a lot of respect."

Resham's admiration for Shantanu grew at that very

moment. They began meeting for Aarti's sake quite frequently and soon she grew to like him. The liking slowly transformed into love and it was not long before the two of them decided to get married, much to the happiness of Aarti. However, they had taken a strong decision – they would not have their own biological child.

When Resham informed her parents about her desire to marry Shantanu and the vow she had taken, they were flummoxed. They could not digest the fact that their daughter was not willing to have her own biological child. It took a lot of time for her to convince them.

"Now that you know the whole story, would you return to Patiala to celebrate our little happiness with us?" Resham asked her pleadingly.

Monika loved Resham and wanted to be with her for sure. However, she surely did not wish to return to Patiala. The memories, which she had carefully buried in the deepest corners of her heart, might get inflamed and she was afraid of that.

That night she could not sleep. She could feel the reflections of every incident. Except Resham, there was no one whose thoughts could bring her some cheer.

However, Resham had also decided not to leave her alone and she kept calling her every night, till she finally gave in. Roopam and Shekhar were also going and she had company.

The bewilderment and turmoil in her mind remained though, even while she was packing her things. Resham asked her, "What will you wear? You are the bride's best friend?"

She replied, "Roopam, I have really no interest in dressing up. Once upon a time, I did have and I loved the traditional dresses – the *ghaghras*, the *saris* and the *anarkalis*. But jeans are what I have now."

Roopam smiled and said, "See, what your brother Shekhar has brought for you..."

Shekhar presented her a nicely wrapped dress. She opened it to find that it was a baby pink stylish *ghaghra* with a blue *chunni*. Shekhar said, "I am sure that you will look even more beautiful than the bride. After all, you are my sister!" and hugged her.

Her eyes were damp once again. She had lost so much in her journey from Patiala to Paris, but she had also gained a lot. For a moment, she wondered if the gain was larger than the loss! The persons she had lost in the voyage were those who never meant anything to her, but being naïve, she had thought that they were her world. And she had gained the love of persons, such as Paul and Shekhar. The number never mattered; the feelings did. And she knew that these were the persons who would always be with her.

□

36

Exit

Shipra had been rather vocal about her protests every now and then and it unsettled Poonam. As soon as they returned from Delhi, after leaving Monika, she decided to broach the subject with Varun once again. She had mentioned about it once to her husband, but he had simply let it pass.

However, some of the guests had not yet left their house, including two of her sister-in-laws, which was a matter of grave concern. She thought it better to wait for a little while till they left.

When they didn't leave even after a week, she was puzzled. In the evening, after dinner, she told her husband, "I want your attention on two issues."

He was also worried about his sisters and knew that it required immediate attention. He was sure that his wife would discuss the same thing and he said, "I know one of the things for sure. Go and ask my sisters what they want before leaving for home.."

She replied, "I am sure that they will ask for a huge amount."

He sighed, "I am aware of that, but then, we will have to face it some day or the other. Why not now?"

Poonam went to Nehali first and then Snehali and invited both of them to her room. After all four of them were seated,

Varun asked, "My dear sisters, I was wondering what gift I should buy for both of you as well as my other sister, Sonali..."

Nehali cackled, "So, you are smart, brother! We all know how you got the entire wealth from Arun. However, you can't swallow the entire riches alone. We need our share."

Snehali added, "We were only waiting for Monika to go away, as were you. Now that things are clear cut with you, we would be happy to have our share."

He watched his sisters intently. They were indeed quite shrewd – much more cunning than he had expected them to be. He could easily plot to eliminate them, but that would raise a finger. He decided that it was best to negotiate with them.

They started with demanding an equal share for all four of them. However, after a lot of discussions, arguments and counter arguments, it was finalised that while fifty per cent of the share would be retained by Varun, the remaining fifty per cent would be equally shared by the three sisters.

After Nehali and Snehali left, Poonam asked, "Will Monika get nothing? Didn't she deserve much more? Rather than negotiating with your sisters, why didn't you negotiate with her?"

He said angrily, "You are intelligent, but then, you are a woman! How can we discuss with Monika? She got what her father left and what remains is ours. I had explained to you all that long before."

She asked, "What about the bungalow? What if she comes and asks us for the same one day?"

He replied, "She won't!"

She asked, "Why?"

He said, "I have silenced the mouth of her husband by giving them one crore."

She looked at him perplexed. There were things beyond her comprehension.

Just then there was a call on Varun's mobile. It was an international call and when he lifted it, it was Monika. She was calling them only for the second time since she had left

India, but she sounded panicky. Her voice was clear to Poonam also who was sitting at a little distance. She said, "*Chacha*... *chacha*...he has vanished...he is not there...I have searched him everywhere..."

He asked, "What do you mean by vanish?"

She replied, "He ditched me, *chacha*, he ditched me. He left me at a Metro station. I have been to the hotel where we stayed. He has already vacated it. Neither does he own the apartment which he told he did, nor does he have a job with Deere International. I am calling from Deere's office. Where do I go *chacha* in this foreign land where I have no friends or anyone else?"

He questioned, "What about the traveller's cheques that I gave you?"

She was quiet for a moment. He could hear her sobs in between. He asked again, a bit louder this time, "What happened to the traveller's cheques that I gave you?"

"How can you think of money when I am in this situation? Anyway, this happened only after he lured me into giving him the money. I don't have anything with me *chacha*, except two Euros. Please help me, *chacha*, please help me!"

He stated straightforwardly, "Listen, Monika, I gave you everything that belonged to you. One crore was the amount at which I began my business and you know it. I had got it assessed by proper firms and I built upon it. I can't give you anything else now."

She screeched, "*Chacha*, it was not money that I was looking at. It is something more...I didn't know that I was just money for you..."

He also said with disgust, "Okay, I will send you the tickets for your return."

He could hear her sobs till she finally disconnected.

Poonam asked, "What...what happened to Monika?"

He stated angrily, "That guy fooled her and stole all her money. Just how careless could she be? One crore is a big amount!"

She asked, "But...Monika...what she will do in a foreign country all alone?"

He replied disgustingly, "I did offer her return tickets..."

She said, "I don't think the manner in which you offered her was kind...please give her a call again...let me give her a call..."

He handed her the mobile and walked away. She lifted the mobile and dialled the number from which the call was received. However, the call was received by the receptionist and she informed that the girl, who had called, had left. She tried getting in touch with Tanishk, but his mobile was switched off as expected. Though Monika was not her real daughter, she felt attached to her and had grown fond of her. She was a greedy woman by nature, but not to this extent. She asked Varun to try to find out more about her or else lodge a complaint about her. He ignored her and said, "What can we do from here? Let her come back and then I will tackle it."

Just then, a maid came to their room with distress written all over her face. When Poonam asked her what the matter was, she replied, "*Bitiya* is not opening her room. It is locked since morning. She did not come out even for breakfast..."

Poonam rushed to Shipra's room which was indeed locked from outside. The maid was not able to understand the modern locks. She called her on her mobile, which was answered after more than a dozen frantic calls. Shipra replied, "Mom, I have left the house – I don't know if it is Monika's house or your house. Anyway, I have left it for good. I got married to Shivam in the morning – it was a registered marriage and there is no scope for either you or Papa to interfere. We are proceeding to Delhi and the only thing you can give us is some money – that is, only if you care for me. I know that you gave a crore to Monika."

Poonam felt the entire world come crashing down. Everything appeared dark and murky. She would have fallen down, had she not been given support by two hands. Gathering her in his hands, Varun took her to their room and called for some glucose water. After she had steadied herself, she told him about Shipra.

He said sadly, "You had been warning me about her since so long, but I didn't take the matter seriously. Let me find out if she is really married or she is just testing our patience."

It was soon confirmed that she had indeed married Shivam. He asked Poonam to give her a call and call her home with him. They arranged for a quick reception, though both of them were not happy with the marriage. When the time came for her departure, Shipra asked Poonam, "What happened to the money you were to give us?"

Varun looked at his balance sheet and gave her a cheque of twenty-five lakhs. She said sharply, "So you love me one-fourth of what you love Monika?"

Varun remained silent, but Poonam said, "Shipra, how can you compare yourself to Monika? You are both so different... you are my daughter and she is like a daughter..."

She said astutely once again, "But she came with money – isn't it? And that satisfied your greed. I am ashamed to have such avaricious parents. Nevertheless, I am your daughter and I won't leave you. I want my share of a crore..."

Poonam stated, "Shipra, why do you behave like this? You do know that whatever belongs to us belongs to you and Ritesh...."

She laughed loudly and said, "The point is that you are living in a dream. The money never belonged to you. I shall take my share till you have it with you. I won't leave even a single rupee...." Holding Shivam's hand, she walked away. Other than the cheque she did not take anything else. She even refused to go in a car which they offered. The newlyweds simply rushed away in an auto.

□

37

Ritesh's Vanishing Trick

Poonam sat sullenly on the sofa after Shipra had left. Varun also came and sat next to her with a heavy heart. Since the time Shipra had left their house to get married to a guy who was neither well educated nor well placed, he felt disheartened. The edifice on which he had carefully built his building was crumbling, each splinter hitting him hard on his face.

However, seeing the condition of Poonam, he forgot his own grief for a moment and said, "Cheer up, Poonam! Shipra is bound to realise her folly, sooner or later."

She stated, "There is nothing to cheer up! At least Shipra was vocal and I always knew what the devil in her mind was thinking. I wonder what goes on in the devilish mind of Ritesh. When he was not available during Monika's wedding, I didn't feel much. If you had observed, he was absent most of the times even during Shipra's reception. I felt that he knew what Shipra was planning and supported her!"

He sat pensively. After some time, he removed his spectacles from his eyes and kept them on the side table. His eyes were moist. He wiped them with his handkerchief and leaning on his wife's shoulders, said, "Poonam, was I wrong somewhere? But...but I did everything in consultation with you...you knew where exactly we were going, didn't you?"

Putting one of her hands over his head, she said, "Yes, you

always considered me as a partner in everything and I was always well informed. However, today I feel that we both made a mistake somewhere...we tried to do the best for our kids, even at the cost of...at the cost of...but...I wonder if our path was correct..."

He suddenly got up and asked, "Poonam....you will never leave my side *naa*? Do you promise that you will always be with me whatever happens?"

She replied, "That goes without saying. The moment I married you, I promised to be with you in good or in bad. And I shall always be with you till my death."

Just then, the bell rang. Poonam got up to open the door. Varun asked, "Where are all the servants?"

She replied, "Today, I gave an off to everyone. I wished to spend some time alone with you and Ritesh, in case he came home. It has been ages since we last sat alone. I believe it was long before we moved to Patiala."

She was happy to see Ritesh when she opened the door. She hugged him tight. He was taken aback and he struggled to move away from her embrace. She asked, "What happened, Ritesh? Can't a mother cuddle her own child?"

He replied rather uncourteously, "I am happy that you have realised that I am your son. Nevertheless, it is too late for that. Please let me go."

Varun shouted, "Please talk properly to your mother... otherwise...otherwise..."

Ritesh asked, "What will you do otherwise? Throw me outside? Remove my name from the property? As if I care for your property! As such I am leaving tomorrow. I was only waiting for Shipra to get married."

Varun confronted him, "You are leaving? Where are you going? Do you think we will allow you to go away?"

He replied, "Mr. Bajaj! I know very well what you did to get this property which belonged to your brother and to what level you stooped. I had overheard the conversation you had with the man called Angad back home. Though I was a child,

I was devastated to know what you had planned. Since then, I have not been myself. I have never really been able to come out of it. I have been planning to move out of your circle of influence since then. I am leaving tomorrow for Dubai where I have my own business plans. I don't want to have anything to do with you or your wife, since she was a party to everything. I hate you...I hate you...I hate you..." and he ran away from there into the confines of his room. Both Poonam as well as Varun kept knocking at his door but to no avail. They could only hear his sobs from inside.

In the morning, while Poonam and Varun still sat on the sofa, they saw him coming out and they rushed towards him. Their gaze was locked for some time. Poonam saw that his long and curly hair was ruffled. His eyes spoke of a pain that she had failed to recognise in the insanity of life. He touched their feet silently and left. None of them had the courage to halt him or even ask him if he would keep in touch. They did not even dare to ask him if he needed money or any other help. They only saw his tall body diminish slowly, till it transformed into a dot which was erased soon after.

That day, Varun did not go for work. He had neither the desire nor the energy left in him. He lay on the sofa in the guestroom and kept wondering about the past. His glance fell upon the actual-size photos of his *bhaiya* and *bhabhi*. He prostrated before the photos and said again and again, "I have sinned. I have sinned. Please show me the right path."

He was so lost in his own grief that he did not realise that Poonam had not spoken to him since the time Ritesh had left. She had not even asked him for tea. He understood her grief completely. After all, he alone was responsible for it. She had simply followed the path shown by him, believing him to be always right.

He called her aloud. When there was no answer, he rushed to the bedroom. When he didn't find her there, he began searching for her madly, all over the house. Finally, he located her in Monika's room. She was dozing on her recliner.

He said with a smile, "Poonam, what a place to rest! I must have searched you all over the house!"

However, when there was no reaction from her, he touched her forehead. It seemed lifeless. He tried to feel her pulse. It was as dead as ice. He screamed, "You...you can't do this, Poonam! You had promised to be my companion your entire life!"

And then, he remembered. She had said, "The moment I married you, I promised to be with you in good or in bad. And I shall always be with you till my death." She was no longer alive to be his companion. She was dead.

He did summon the doctors immediately, but as expected, they only asserted that she was no more.

As she was decorated as a bride, he felt that he was dead too. The last thread to his connection with life had broken. He could not really summon the courage to lift her dead body on his shoulder. He was dead for all practical purposes and participated in all the rituals like a machine.

Shipra did come with Shivam on being informed, but there was no way in which he could inform Ritesh. He also comprehended the attachment she had with Monika as he could recollect what she had said when he had last heard from Monika, but she was lost to him. Somewhere down the line, he had a belief that Monika would come home someday. His heart belonged to Poonam and he wished to join her in heaven. But for that, he had to wait till he handed over everything to the rightful owner – Monika.

In the week that followed, he sold off the company and deposited all the money in the bank in Monika's name. Shipra did keep pestering him for money and left disgusted and dissatisfied, but he did not care. He sold off his own house and sent all the money to Shipra. After that, he took to the couch. The doctors could not diagnose anything, but he never got up after that. The servants could only hear him murmur something the whole day and entire night. His closest servant, Ramdeen, even told everyone that he never slept. The only words that he found audible were "Resham, please call Monika," and he decided to call Resham.

At that point of time, even Resham did not know where Monika was and could do nothing. However, even after she got in touch with Monika and informed her, Monika had no desire to meet him, talk to him or talk about him. She did not allow Resham to even mention his name. As far as she was concerned, he was dead for her long back and she had banned his mention, just as she had made her promise that she would not speak of Gurpreet.

□

38

A Chance Meeting

True to his words, Gurpreet had not married. The only thing he had done was to take to drinking. He was a teetotaler till the incidents in his life changed him.

He was very much in love with Monika and wanted to marry her. However, a meeting with Mr. Shukla had convinced him that it was beneficial for both of them not to marry each other. At least, if Monika married Tanishk, her life was safe. His adoration of her had finally made him take the extreme decision of convincing Monika that it was best for her to marry Tanishk. He still remembered the day when he had got a call from a private number. The voice at the other end said, "I am S.S. Shukla. Can you meet me at my house? It is urgent and related to Monika. I am her father's friend."

Gurpreet had read a lot about the uprightness of Mr. Shukla, who had been the DCP of Patiala. He rushed to his house.

Mr. Shukla questioned, "Are you in love with Monika?"

He did not know what he was expected to reply. He said honestly, "Yes, uncle. I wish to marry her."

Mr. Shukla stated, "If you really love her, don't marry her unless her uncle agrees."

He asked, "Why, uncle? We both love each other and…"

Mr. Shukla explained, "There are things under investigation. I have a strong suspicion to link her uncle to her family's untimely death. However, the investigation could not be completed and I was transferred out. Since then, I have been kept away from Patiala. There is no one else who can chase the case and the file lies untouched."

He exclaimed, "We can raise the issue. I will pursue it till a logical end is reached and the culprits are caught."

Looking at him intently, Mr. Shukla said, "It is not very easy, Gurpreet. Remember that Monika stays with them. A wrong move on our part could mean much more for her. If you really love her, just leave her to be married to the person they have chosen for her. I can't reveal more than this at this stage."

Gurpreet could not understand the details which led Mr. Shukla belief that Monika's life was in danger. However, he understood his concern. While he was wondering what he should do, his father came into his room. When he saw his son so nervous, he was worried and asked him about it. After hearing him, he said, "Let me try something. I will go to Monika's house and request her uncle to get the two of you married."

Gurpreet asked, "What if he refuses you? What if he insults you?"

His father stated, "Then we will know that we did try our best. I am not as much vexed about my insults as I am about the future of both of you."

Just after his father left, he got a call from Tanishk, informing him about Monika's suicide attempt. He was completely dumbfounded. Words refused to come out from his mouth. However, he had to be strong – if not for his own sake, for Monika's sake. He got up with great difficulty and went to the hospital to face her and explain her why marrying Tanishk would be the best for her, without letting her know the details about his meeting with Mr. Shukla.

When Monika asked him to run away and start life afresh,

he craved to tell her that he indeed wished to do that. However, it was with much difficulty that he told her that his parents had gone to meet her uncle and in case they wouldn't agree, it was best for both of them to part. He had hoped that Monika would be able to face everything well. As expected, her uncle had refused marriage with Gurpreet. He had felt devastated, but borne it all silently. His vow not to marry anyone else but Monika was firm.

With a heavy heart, he had gone for her marriage, but was sad to see the behaviour of Tanishk's relatives with Monika. It was for the first time he wondered if he had been right in asking Monika to marry him. When he had heard about what Monika had to undergo in Paris, he was shocked. He had often asked Resham to intervene and give her address so that he could rush to her. He knew how much she needed him. However, Monika had maintained a stoic silence and forced Resham to promise that she would neither discuss Gurpreet with her nor tell him anything about her.

Not able to bear his guilt in letting Monika marry Tanishk, he had taken to heavy drinking in the evening. That particular day, he had gone to Ludhiana on a business tour. He had to stay over for the next part of negotiations, so he went down to the bar. Seated just next to him was another person wearing almost the same attire as him – a black turban, an off-white shirt and a black coat. Both of them ordered a Johnnie Walker at the same time. The other guy shook hands with Gurpreet and said, "Angad."

He replied, "Gurpreet."

While both of them sat silently, Gurpreet kept ordering peg after peg as Angad watched. Angad was also a heavy drinker, but Gurpreet had crossed all limits. He asked Gurpreet, "Is it a girl?"

He was in an inebriated condition and he replied, "Oh, yes! Love makes one what I have become...I loved her so much...so much...so much..."

Angad asked, "Then, what happened then?"

He replied, "How will you understand unless you have been in love? I loved her, she loved me and yet I did not marry her...rather, I could not marry her...." he began sobbing.

Comforting him, Angad asked, "Who was the girl? I can get any girl to your toes...rather, I can do anything – from murder to lifting the girl...just tell me who is it and where she is...I will get her for you...it is a promise...."

Gurpreet stated, "No one can get her...no one...." Then staring at him he asked, "Why this sudden sympathy for me? You do not even know me!"

Angad laughed, "Ha...ha...ha...I sort of liked you. And these drinks...they make strange companions...tell me who the girl is? And she will be here..."

Gurpreet had never before taken her name anytime, but that particular day, it slipped out of his tongue, "No one can get Monika...she is in Paris, far away from me...far away from everyone..."

Looking at him intently, Angad asked, "You mean Monika Bajaj? From Patiala?"

Gurpreet nodded his head. Angad cackled all of a sudden and said, "Although this girl is mad, she indeed has a charm – you know, I was also carried away by her once upon a time... shall I tell what all I did to get her?"

The drunkenness of Gurpreet was pushed behind and he looked attentively at the guy sitting next to him. He tried to recollect if Monika had ever mentioned anything about the guy. And then he remembered. Just before her parent's death, they had received a proposal from this guy asking for Monika's hand. Later he had married their family friend, Dr. Khosla's daughter. His attention was aroused. He ordered whisky for the both of them. Though Angad continued to drink, he stopped. He took out his mobile stealthily and pressed the record button.

Angad talked of unimportant things for some time;

however, after the drink had its effect, he began narrating in broken sentences, "You know – I saw this girl in a marriage and I fell heads and heels over her. Unaware of my attention, she continued with her activities. There never had been a girl who had not paid any attention to me and she interested me a lot. I immediately approached her *chacha* who was known well to me."

Angad was drinking again. Gurpreet wished that he would speak faster, but he knew that there would be no use asking him. He was a man of his own desires. After he had taken another peg, he continued, "I was a big exporter of leather and the richest person in the area. I would get proposals for marriage from so many families. However, when her uncle approached this girl's father, he flatly refused. This irked me."

He continued to drink. After he had two more pegs, he stated, "A refusal arouses nasty things in me. I became a devil. I decided to teach her father a lesson. I began competing with him in all the tenders that he participated in. I even meddled with the contracts he already had entered into, mostly by crook. I wanted him to come to me on his knees to get his daughter married to me. But that man was quite stubborn. He refused to yield despite that. Finally, I eliminated him."

Gurpreet saw that Angad was not in his senses at all by then. He asked him, "It must have been difficult to eliminate him, isn't it?"

Angad chuckled, "It was the easiest. He was going with his family to a marriage. One of my trucks crushed their car."

Gurpreet asked, "Did you finally marry the girl?"

Taking another peg, Angad explained, "By that time, another girl had caught my interest. She was much more beautiful than this Monika of yours. Moreover, her uncle informed me that she was only beautiful to look at but was mentally ill and suffered from schizophrenia. Such girls are good for a one-night stand, but certainly not good enough to be married. My wife is alright, but I have lost interest in her too. I have had many girlfriends. Money lures them to me. While I decide which girl to have at which point of time, this time my girlfriend left me...I will teach her a lesson..."

Gurpreet was shaken. He wanted to beat him black and blue, but better sense prevailed. Leaving him there in his condition, he rushed back to Patiala. On his way, he gave a call to Mr. Shukla, informing him of the latest development.

□

39

The Deceit Gets Revealed

The case of the murder of Mr. Bajaj, his wife and his son was reopened, thanks to Gurpreet's efforts. He posted the audio on all social networking sites and soon it was made viral. There was no option left to the police other than to register the case.

Death threats were issued to Gurpreet, but he did not care. It was a case of justice for his dearest Monika, whom he valued more than his own life. The thought that she had been suffering in Paris had never left him. As far as he knew her, she would not find solace in anything other than love. He did hear that she was expanding her horizons, but a part of him said that she was still a little girl.

One day, while he was sitting at the police station, he saw a group of hooligans being brought for eve teasing. He would not have paid much attention to the group had he not recognised one of them as the one who had troubled Monika during her marriage. He had been made to apologise to him by Monika, since they were Tanishk's relatives.

Gurpreet knew the Police Inspector quite well by now and asked him if he could speak to that guy. The Police Inspector was kind enough to allow him and facing him at the lock-up, he asked, "What is your name, friend?"

Looking at him interrogatingly, he said, "Robin. Why?"

Gurpreet passed on a thousand rupee note and replied, "I think we met at a marriage. Tanishk Monga's marriage."

He chuckled, "I go to marriages and party rallies and wherever you take me for money. If you wish, I can come with you and also get my friends. You will have to promise me good food and drinks besides the money."

Gurpreet enquired, "Think hard. This was a marriage at the Bajaj household. It was quite a lavish marriage and was talked about a lot."

He chortled, "Oh yes! I remember! We had a nice time teasing the bride at that marriage. The food was really yummy and we got the best of whisky. I haven't had such a drink after that."

Gurpreet questioned, "Robin, was the bridegroom related to you?"

He snickered, "I want money for this answer."

Gurpreet gave him another note of thousand rupees. He answered, "No, I was not related to the bridegroom. None of us were. We were all hired by him."

This explained him a lot of things. Everything was well planned by the guy called Tanishk. Gurpreet was very annoyed. He decided to confront Monika's *chacha*. He wanted to find out if he was also involved in the deceit played upon Monika during her marriage or if he was simply uninvolved. His connection to Monika's parent's death had been evident and the police was going to question him soon. But this was an answer which he wanted for himself and Monika.

Gurpreet reached Monika's house after long. The bungalow which spoke of all the splendours once upon a time was barren and dark. There were cobwebs all around. Though it was already dark, he could not find any lights. He tried to locate the call-bell, but it was broken. The door was half-open. He knocked at the door. A servant came out and asked him who he was. He replied, "I am Gurpreet and I have come to meet Mr. Bajaj."

The servant stated, "Come in. We don't get guests and I

think my master will be happy to have one. In case, you knew him before, let me warn you that he hardly recognises anyone these days. He even failed to recognise his own daughter the last fortnight. He is only counting days and waiting for someone to return – I can't say who it is."

Led by the servant, Gurpreet entered Mr. Bajaj's room. The grandeur, which the bungalow was so much known for, was conspicuous by its absence. His room was also dimly lit. The room was void of all decorations, almost as if it had been stripped naked. Mr. Bajaj lay, not on a bed, but on a simple *charpoy*. He had become extremely frail and thin. His bones peeped out from his body just like the stems on a creeper when it is no longer a flowering season. The retinae of his eyes were purged inside and they were red. Hearing his footsteps, he asked, "Have you come over, Monika?"

Gurpreet replied, "It is me – Gurpreet."

Mr. Bajaj burst out crying. He murmured a few words in a voice weak enough to be heard. The only thing he could make out was his sobs. Gesturing him to sit, Mr. Bajaj asked his servant to fetch something and he returned with a diary. Handing him the diary, Mr. Bajaj again murmured something which was inaudible. His servant said, "He says that all his actions have been stated in the diary and he is ready to receive any punishment for his actions."

Gurpreet had gone there to confront Mr. Bajaj, but seeing his condition, he was not sure of going ahead with it. Seeing him hesitate, Mr. Bajaj again uttered a few words and began sobbing. His servant stated, "He is saying that he is extremely sorry for the injustice he has meted out to you. The diary has proof of everything and you can hand over the same to the police so that he is punished. If you know where Monika is, please get her back so that he can die in peace."

Gurpreet was puzzled. He wondered where his wife and children were. He wondered how he had recognised him. His servant had told him earlier that he had not even identified his own daughter. Nevertheless, he returned home with the diary.

Once at home, he read the diary, page by page. It had details right from the beginning since Monika's *chacha* and *chachi* had come to her parents with a marriage proposal for Angad. That time, his simple aim was to extract money from Angad for the union. However, as things complicated, his participation also convoluted and he became party to conniving the murder of his own brother. If Angad was the chief conspirator, he was a completely involved party and participated with full consciousness.

By the time he shifted to Monika's house, his mind had fully corrupted. Having gained access to the entire business and the bungalow, he had decided to eliminate Angad from the scene and had even plotted for the same, but it was sheer luck that he had lost interest in Monika by then. He simply spread the rumour that Monika was schizophrenic.

His next task was to take over the reins of the business. He knew fully well that his brother also wished that Monika should lead the business. With the help of his wife, he ensured that she lost interest in business. He also got the business valued so that no one could raise a finger at him. The next task was to send Monika away. For this, he was looking for a guy who would take her away and Tanishk provided the right opportunity. He was so busy in sending away Monika, that he did not even verify the credentials of Tanishk, who turned out to be a much bigger scoundrel and deprived him of a crore worth of money.

While running after money, what he forgot was that he had also neglected his own children. Both of them revolted against him and his wife in their own way and ran away, leaving them forlorn and alone forever. He finished the entries in his diary by stating, "I have been a bastard and I deserve all the punishment. I would have ended my life, but I am waiting for Monika to return so that I can hand her everything and leave this world. However, I wish my diary to be publicised so that no one does the kind of things I did."

Gurpreet's father entered the room at that moment and

he handed over the diary to him. After reading the contents, he said, "I think that the old man has already been punished by God. Today, I am sure that there is something called justice. Money can boost the ego of people and make them torment the world, but He sees that all tyrants are given the punishment they deserve."

Gurpreet asked, "But I do wish Angad to be sent to prison. He was the one who killed Monika's parents."

His father replied, "You can't be selective. If you use this diary, Monika's uncle will also be dragged to court. However, there is good news for you. Mr. Shukla called to inform that the guy who was driving the truck when Monika's parents were killed has been caught and he has accepted his crime."

Gurpreet hugged his father and said, "That really makes me ecstatic. Both the crooks have been hounded. Angad will soon be reeling in prison and Monika's uncle is almost on his death-bed."

His father said, "Let us go to Paris, son! I am sure that we will be able to locate Monika. She will be so happy to hear all this. I don't suppose she knows anything about the conspiracies."

He answered, "*Papa*! She is coming here for Resham's marriage."

□

40

The Journey to Patiala

When Monika, along with Shekhar and Roopam, boarded the flight to go back to India, she was unsure of her feelings. She was still afraid of meeting her old friends and reconnecting to her past. In Paris, she had been insulated from everything, but the flight brought forth all the memories safely hidden in the crevices of her heart. She recollected how she had boarded her first flight as a coy bride about to rejoin her husband and how she had been welcomed with open arms by Tanishk. Her entire body burnt in rage at the thought of him. She hated those kisses that he had taken, she loathed her body for having been touched by him and she scorned her mind for having believed in him. She even detested Gurpreet for having asked her to marry Tanishk. She reviled the money her father had left for her. If only she had no money, she would have been leading a happy life and may be, would have got married to Gurpreet and had a few kids. The thought of kids made her blush. She had always loved kids and how she wished that she had at least one daughter! She saw a couple with a little girl about three-to-four years old. The girl was continuously pestering her parents with her silly questions while they tried their best to answer her. She smiled at the girl. The girl threw a flying kiss at her and she reciprocated back. Children are such a wonderful reason to live for. She wondered if she would ever have one.

"Do you mind if I take the corner seat?" It was Roopam, who was asking her this question and she was brought back into the present. She stated with a smile, "For a would-be mother, everything is permitted. You don't have to ask, just order."

While Roopam took the window seat, Shekhar sat on the middle seat and she on the aisle seat. She remembered that she had taken an aisle seat even while going to Paris. Her mind was trying to find similarities and differences in the two journeys and she wondered why it was happening like that. She tried to bury herself in a magazine. She did not even lift her face when the plane took up. It was only after the steward asked her, "What would you like to have, Madam?" did she raise her head. She ordered some tomato juice and was holding the glass in her hand and sipping it, when her glance fell upon the seat just in front of their row, but in the other direction. The hair, the gait, the voice – everything was the same. She could not believe that she had even made love to this person, leave alone touching him. She found the entire act despicable. She hated her body and her mind for having accepted him. For a moment, she could not move. She wondered if she had indeed seen him. It was Tanishk indeed! Or Animesh...or whatever he called himself now...

She whispered in Shekhar's ears, "It is him!"

He asked her, "Him means?" He could not connect.

She said again, "It is the guy who married me and fooled me...and then ditched me after he had my money..."

He looked at him. He was busy giving attention to another girl sitting next to him. Both of them glanced at the girl. She was another Indian girl, beautiful to look at. She was wearing a *mangalsutra* and had also put on *sindoor* in the parting on her forehead. He asked her once again, "Are you sure?"

"Hundred per cent sure, Shekhar. I spent my days with him. I can never forget that bastard," she replied.

He asked her to take the middle seat which he had occupied a little while ago and advising her to keep her face hidden behind the magazine, got up and approached the crew. After showing the head crew his identity card, he informed them about the guy and his case for which he had already lodged an F.I.R. He had kept the scanned copy on his mobile. The crew informed to him that the guy's name was Utkarsh Singh. His destination was Munich, which was the next destination of the flight. She assured him that suitable action would be taken against him as soon as they landed at Munich and she would be in touch with the air control.

All three of them waited with abated breaths till they reached Munich. She did not even go to the washroom despite feeling the need. Finally, after the plane landed, an announcement was made by the crew, "In view of some issues at the airport, the guests can leave the flight only after we receive a clearance. Don't worry; it shall not take more than an hour."

There was a lot of pandemonium on the flight. Those who wished to get down had stood up. Tiny tots cried. The three of them sat wondering if their request had been heeded to. Finally, after almost twenty minutes, the police streamed inside the flight. This finally brought a smile on her lips. She removed the magazine in front of her face. The police went straight to his seat and asked him to stand up.

He argued, "What have I done? You are pestering a passenger for no reason and no fault. I have the passport, the visa and everything else that you may need. You can inspect my documents."

All the passengers on the flight were astounded and wondered what was going on. The lady sitting next to him began to cry and howl, "How can you hound my husband? He has done nothing!"

It was at this moment that Monika could not restrain herself. Standing up, she addressed everyone, "Friends, this is a guy who marries girls from India, gets them here to this continent and then leaves them to their fate after having taken everything from her." Addressing the girl, she asked, "Would you have liked to be ditched by your so-called husband after you reached your destination – or do you think it is better to have known about him and be saved now?"

The girl looked around in disbelief, while Monika handed her the copy of the F.I.R which she always carried with her. It had a photo of Monika with the guy and the girl understood that a treachery had been played upon her too.

By that time, the police had handcuffed Tanishk and was taking him away. Since the time he had seen Monika, he had known that his game was over. Monika watched him being taken away by the German police, who were really well-built and taller than him. She felt that justice had finally been done. Somehow, she had confidence that he would land up in jail. After all, she had all the proof. And she was also certain that when the case would become a newspaper report, many other girls would also come out with harrowing tales of having been deceived by him.

The girl, who was with Tanishk, looked around helplessly. A sense of love was aroused in Monika, who asked Shekhar to help her.

Shekhar gave her the number of one of his friends in the German Embassy and also of another friend staying in Munich and asked her to get in touch with them. He called up both of them and explained the circumstances in which the girl would be contacting them. The girl also got down at Munich along with the other passengers.

Soon, the flight took off. There were no halts after Munich till they reached Delhi, from where they had to take another flight to Chandigarh. Monika felt really light in her head. She chatted freely with Shekhar and Roopam after that. When the two of them dozed, she read a magazine. However, her thoughts flew to Patiala and her good old days. For the first time, she was looking forward to the marriage.

Monika was thrilled as she saw the flight land at the Indira Gandhi Terminal in Delhi. Their flight to Patiala was five hours later. She told Shekhar, "I want to go shopping!"

The three of them went to the nearest market. Shekhar and Roopam watched her enthusiasm in purchasing everything Indian – the saris, the suits and the accessories and they smiled. Shekhar said, "I think Monika is finally happy now. I sincerely hope that she agrees to meet Gurpreet. I am sure that he will convince her and they will always be happy together."

Roopam replied, "It is not so easy, Shekhar. As far as I know Monika, she is quite head-strong. She has suffered a lot in life and she will never agree."

Shekhar said, "Okay, let us take a bet!"

□

41

Meeting with Gurpreet

Roopam's parents had come to receive them at Chandigarh. Her mother embraced Monika before embracing her own daughter and said, "The shine of Patiala had gone away for long and it is a pleasure to have you back." Monika was touched by this kind gesture. This is what she had been missing in Paris.

On her way to Patiala, she saw with eagerness the area around. The yield in the fields was not so high, the roads were dirty and the traffic was chaotic – and yet, she loved it. Everything looked as if it was her own. Even the moon, which was slowly making its appearance, appeared hers. She remembered the time when her father would take her in his lap and tell her numerous poems about the moon. Earlier, his memories would give her pain and make her eyes moist; now, they brought a smile. She was lucky to have had such lovely parents.

Resham's house had been nicely decorated. The initial phase of reluctance in getting her married to Shantanu had melted away and it was replaced by fervour for the event. He seemed to have invaded the hearts of her parents. Roopam and Monika wished to meet Shantanu immediately. He had snatched away the heart of their loved one and had to be special. However, the functions prohibited his entry into the house till marriage and they decided to meet him in a restaurant. When they informed Resham of their plan, she told Monika, "While returning, do meet your *chacha*. He is on his death-bed and keeps uttering your name all the time."

She said with disgust, "Let it be, Resham. Leave alone meeting, I will not talk about any of my relatives. The moment you utter that once again, I will go away from here."

When they approached the gate of the restaurant, Roopam said, "Monika, I completely forgot! Since I am the sister-in-law of Shantanu, I should have got some gift for him. I will just get something from the opposite shop while you introduce yourself to Shantanu."

When she stepped inside, Monika was taken aback. The person sitting right in front of her was Gurpreet and not Shantanu. Their glance met for a fraction of a second, and she decided to run away; but he was faster than her. Holding her wrist, he said, "Monika, please sit with me for a few minutes. If for nothing else, than at least for old times' sake."

Everyone was watching them and she had no option. She followed him to his table. Looking at her intently, he said, "Monika, please accept my apologies for every mishap that you faced. I know that I am the culprit and I understand that no amount of apologies can erase what you went through."

She said, "I have come here to meet Shantanu and please let me go now."

He continued, "Monika! Shantanu will come after half an hour. This was planned by me in association with him and Roopam."

She strove to get up and go, but he put his feet over hers. She finally asked angrily, "What do you want from me?"

He replied, "Nothing! I only wish you to hear me out."

She was silent for some time. Then she stated, "We can't talk anything personal in this restaurant. People will hear. They are already watching through the corner of their eyes."

He asked, "Can I invite you home?"

He noticed that she was not replying to any of his questions immediately, but only after a gap. She was not the same old shy Monika now, but a confident Monika and he liked her all the more in this new avatar. She questioned, "What about your wife? Have you asked her?"

He cackled, "Monika, I had promised you that I will either marry you or nobody and I have kept my promise. There is no one home."

Finally after he had cleared a lot of her doubts, she agreed to accompany him to his house. He still had his old car, a Mercedes in which she had enjoyed many a rides. She was taken back in time when he had kissed her in this car and Shipra had seen them. Anyway, that was in the past. She tried her best to erase the inrush of memories. She said to herself, 'Let me hear out what he wishes to say. After that, I will have nothing to do with him.'

The door of his house was locked, as expected. After he opened the door and she entered inside, she was surprised to see that everything was exactly at the same place as it had been when she used to frequent the house. The only change was a photo hanging on the wall. She looked amazingly at the photo and then at Gurpreet. It was her photo! He stated, "She is the girl whom I have always loved and worshipped. If I tell you the incidents which occurred, you might understand why I let her go away that time."

Asking her to sit, he made some ginger tea for her as he knew that she loved it. As she sipped it, she remembered how much she used to enjoy tea made by him. Finally, he handed over the diary of her *chacha* and said, "Do read this. I will tell you the remaining part of the story later. It is quite a horrifying history of the incidents that followed the proposal received by your father from Angad."

She asked, "How did you manage to get this diary?"

He replied, "Your *chacha* gave it to me. I had gone to his house to question him and get him penalised for everything that he had done, but he is already on his death-bed, waiting for you."

She interrogated, "But why did you go to him?"

He said, "Okay! Let me explain right from the beginning. I am sure that you were not convinced when I told you to get married to Tanishk. I could not even look at your eyes when I had to refuse your suggestion to run away and get married since your guardians were not permitting our marriage. But I had reasons to believe that it was the safest path for you. Your uncle, Mr. Shukla had summoned me and cautioned me about the safety of your life in case you got married to someone your *chacha* did not support." He explained to her the proceedings of his meeting with Mr. Shukla in detail and after that asked her to read the diary.

As she read the diary, line by line and word by word, she was more and more dumbfounded. She simply could not comprehend how money can corrupt someone to a level her *chacha* had stooped! When she read the page wherein it was stated that her parents' death was preplanned and well-executed, she shuddered. Tears filled her eyes and she cuddled to Gurpreet, saying, "Please say that it is not true...please say it once...just state that nothing in this diary is true..."

He patted her head and stated, "Monika, every bit of it is true. You can ask Shukla uncle in case you don't believe me."

She said, "I can't read a single word. Please spare me."

Gurpreet coaxed her as if she was a small child, "Monika, to comprehend what life is, you have to learn your past. You can't run away from it. I know what occurred was horrible and loathsome. However, you can't get disassociated from it. You will be happy to know that one of the two biggest culprits, Angad, is behind the bars. He was finally caught a week ago. The other - your uncle, awaits death. His wife died due to shock. Your cousin, Ritesh ran away to Dubai and does not maintain any contacts. Shipra keeps pestering your uncle every now and then and is not happy."

She asked innocently, "Does all this bring back my parents and my brother? Will it bring back my youth? Will it transform me into the same old Monika who believed everyone?"

He remained quiet for he had no words. Whatever justice

is imparted by humans is only partial. No, he could not do anything to get her complete and full justice. The only clock he could reset was that of their marriage. He was very much in love with Monika and wished to ask her then and there. He wondered if it was the right time. But then, another thought struck his mind. He had already let her go for long. If he let her vanish once again, who knows if he would get her again?

He whispered softly, "Monika, I...I've been a coward and I've let you suffer a lot. But...I have always loved you. There has been no moment when I didn't think of you. Your love for me has always been unshakable. Can we get married, Monika?"

She looked at him in disbelief and untangled her hands from his. After that, she took a few steps backwards and sprinted away as fast as she could. Gurpreet kept calling her, but she didn't listen. She ran and ran till she reached her house.

□

42
Chacha's Death

While she was rushing away from Gurpreet, what she did not realise was that she was heading not towards Resham's house where she was staying, but towards her own house. When she saw where she had reached, she stood frozen. She wanted to run away from there too, but something made her stop. She kept on gazing at her bungalow with her mouth as well as eyes wide open. The bungalow, which used to be so well-maintained, was almost in tatters. The grandeur of yesteryears was all lost. Patches of paint were peeling off. Soot had deposited all over – mostly from the factory that she could see a few metres behind the bungalow. Weeds had sprouted in the garden and it obscured the view of the main gate and the stairs. A few trees had fallen down, but no one had even bothered to remove the branches. Instead of the roses and other fragrant flowers that used to embellish the garden during those days, there was a stench emanating from the water which had clogged. She hated the sight. She despised the fall of the magnificence of the bungalow.

As if in a trance, she kept walking. She opened the gate of the garden and entered inside. There was a very narrow pathway, with the entire patch of land swarmed with thorny bushes. She was finding it difficult to maintain her balance and yet she walked on. She could see the swing on which she used to sit with her brother while her father pushed them. She could still hear her brother singing nursery rhymes as he swung. Creepers had grown all over the swing, due to disuse. She decided to step further. There was a small piece of land on the way which was muddy and she had to walk really carefully to cross it. Finally, she climbed the three steps which took her to the verandah. She remembered the time when as a little kid, she would try to alight the steps despite falling down every time. She remembered her father's words, "Never give up! Whatever may be the circumstances! Always listen to the heart, for it never lies." She felt like sitting on the steps for a few minutes and she did just that. Only after a little while she got up and pushed the button of the call-bell. It was broken. She knocked. She heard a voice say, "Come in, Monika!"

It was *chacha's* voice. Only a few moments before she had read his diary full of apologies and he was the last person she wished to talk to. However, she walked inside dazedly, wondering how he knew that the person to have come in was her. She stared at him. He lay on the right side of his body. He was nothing but a bundle of bones and looked like a skeleton. His eyes were fixed on the wall which made her wonder if he could see or he had turned blind. He lifted his left hand with a lot of difficulty and touching the palms of both his hands, said, "Monika, I ask for your pardon for everything. I am sure that you must have read my diary and understood what a scoundrel I have been. I am going away and wish to meet you in the other life to show by my actions that I have indeed transformed."

His voice was trembling and almost inaudible, but she could make out what he was saying. After all, she had stayed with him for long. He continued, "Please take out the things under my pillow."

She obeyed without a word. There was a key and a few papers. He said, "I was waiting only to hand over to you both these things. The key is the bungalow's key and then there are the bank papers. I am sorry I could not look after your business empire since the time Poonam left me. Since I had no clue how to contact you and I was too frail to look after it, I sold off everything at the best price and deposited the money in the various schemes of the bank. The deed says that only you can withdraw the money. I promise you that not a single pie has been swindled."

She was still quiet. She was at a complete loss for words. He added, "Monika, give me your hands in my hands and let me hold them."

She followed as was being told. He suddenly began to howl very loudly as he felt them and said, "Please...please take these things and before I go...please marry Gurpreet...he is the best guy you can every have and he loves you like no one else can..."

She closed her eyes. He sobbed for some time and then it was all quiet. His hands seemed to have turned cold. She opened his eyelids and saw that his face wore a blank expression. His pupils were staring at her continuously. Puzzled, she searched for his veins. It was then that she realised that he was dead.

Just then, the servant entered the house. For one moment he looked at her and then at his master. Finally, he said, "So the day of your arrival and his going away has finally come! I knew he had to depart from this world the moment you came...but I am happy that he got to meet you before he left. I was his most trusted servant when he was at Ludhiana and he called me over here after my Madam's death."

Taking out a piece of paper, he said, "These are the contact details of his children, but he had said that they will not come on his death. Anyway, please give them a call."

She began by ringing Ritesh. A female voice, presumably of his wife, received the call and when told him who she was, she handed over the phone to him. After she said who she was, he stated, "I know you, Monika. How have you been?"

She was surprised at his warmth and questioned, "Ritesh... we hardly ever spoke...but *chacha*...I mean...your father has died and I suppose, you should come over..."

He asked her, "Do you really think I should come over,

Monika? Does he deserve anything even during his death? I suppose, you are the best person to answer this question..."

She remained silent. He added, "Leave him to rot. He deserves only that. I am sorry that I was too young to understand your pain that time. My blood used to boil on seeing his actions and his disregard to me and Shipra. Little did I know that all the attention was being given to you so that he could get your money for us. I am ashamed of him. You are my sister and if you ever need me, I will come running. However, I refuse to come for that man called father."

She asked, "What about Shipra?"

He replied, "She is still immature and wants all that money for herself, I suppose. I have tried my best to explain to her, but to no avail. You should not talk to her. I will inform her. However, since she knows that all the riches have been handed over back to you, I suppose she will not come. Wait for her till evening, otherwise you can ask Mangu, our servant to perform the last rites."

Not really understanding what her next step should be, she called up Shekhar, who arrived immediately with Shantanu, Roopam and her parents.

In the evening, *chacha* was taken to the burial site. There were hardly any people. Shipra, as expected, did not come. The last rites were performed by Mangu, as desired by Ritesh.

While the male members went for the last rites, Roopam, her mother and Monika were at the bungalow. Roopam's mother asked, "What will you do with the bungalow now? I suppose you should renovate it and restore its previous glory."

She replied, "Aunty, the glory of the bungalow had vanished with my father's death. It became a place of contention and took away all the happiness and sanguinity of my life. I will not like to stay here even if I decide to return to India someday. Nevertheless, I would like to renovate it and start an NGO if you all will support me."

Roopam asked, "What sort of an NGO do you plan to start?"

She replied, "An NGO sheltering all those women who have no one in the world. We will make it a self-sufficient unit. Trainers will teach them various skills, such as *papad* making, *achaa*r making, knitting, stitching, embroidery etc. so that they earn while they learn. My father has left enough money to begin my work and after that, we will look for finances."

Roopam's mother kissed her on her forehead and said, "God bless you! If you have a dream, you will surely fulfil it. After all, you are a strong girl."

□

43

Resham's Marriage

Resham had been at the beauty parlour, getting ready for her D-day. After she returned home, she came to know of the happenings of the day and was stupefied. Gurpreet had not even told her about those details, since he felt that it was very personal and only Monika could decide who was to be told. She had wondered when Angad was arrested, but was too busy with her own story to find the association.

They discussed at length about Monika's *chacha* and everything else, but she just could not understand her friend's refusal at accepting Gurpreet's proposal. She asked, "Monika, but I still can't understand. Why did you decline Gurpreet? I am sure that you both loved each other."

Monika was mum.

Resham enquired, "Was there someone else at Paris?"

Monika stated, "No, Resham. I did receive a proposal from Paul; but I am far away from love. It is something I stopped trusting long ago. Marriage is simply out of question. Once bitten, twice shy."

Resham asked, "Where is Paul now?"

After Monika informed her that he had dedicated himself to the services of the church, something clicked in Resham's mind and she decided to unite the lovers. She further questioned Monika, "What is it that inhibits you from accepting love? The experiences that you had are something which none of us can erase even if we wish to, but we can surely cover them up with more and more love. Open your heart. Leave yourself free. Let love enter you. I can understand what you went through, but sometime in life one has to believe people. Don't you believe me?"

Monika replied, "That is different. You have been a part of me since long."

Resham asked, "Hasn't Gurpreet been a part of your life for long? Isn't there something about him that you could never forget even while marrying Tanishk? And then, why did you refuse Paul? Monika, you are trying to forcefully hide your love and this is not good either for you or for Gurpreet. Think from his perspective. Hasn't he waited for you since so many years? He could have married after your wedding, but he didn't – only because he loved you. Don't you think he deserves a chance to show you his love for you?"

Monika remained quiet. She wondered if she was indeed not letting herself be free. But the mind refused to listen to her. She knew that Gurpreet loved her and had always loved her. She did realise that she would never get a love like that ever again. And yet, she was afraid – afraid of committing; afraid of falling in love once more; afraid of being ditched. She lay down on the bed in her room and kept brooding for long. And she was sure. She didn't wish to marry – even if it was Gurpreet. She believed him. What she did not believe was her own destiny. The journey from Patiala to Paris had been a long one. She had no energy left to undertake further voyages.

Since the decision had already been taken, Monika decided to unbound herself and enjoy the purpose for which she was here – Resham's marriage. Along with Roopam, she went to the beauty parlour. She was already a beauty – but her skin shone after the visit. She wore the *ghaghra* that Shekhar had presented her.

"You look ravishing!" said Roopam as she came to see her. Together, they went to Resham's room. Decked as a bride, she was gleaming with joy. A little girl came running into the room and hugging Resham, said, "Mom! You look beautiful!"

Monika understood who she was. While she was thinking of introducing herself, Aarti noticed her and exclaimed, "Aren't you the beautiful friend of my Mom from Paris?"

She smiled and hugged her. Aarti was indeed a loveable child and she had further bloomed in Resham's love. They clicked immediately. When the *baraat* came, Gurpreet came up to ask Roopam and Monika to bring the bride down for the *jaimala* ceremony. Monika noticed that he had not looked at her at all even while addressing her.

When they went down with the bride, she could feel Gurpreet's eyes on her, but the moment she looked at him, he changed the direction of his glance. This action was repeated by both of them several times and it was so evident that even Aarti noticed and whispered in her ears, "Gurpreet *mama* is a very nice guy. Is he angry with you for some reason?"

When the bride and the groom sat on the stage, she was asked to accompany them. All this was Resham's plan. Gurpreet was also asked to come over for the photos and somehow their places were next to each other. He didn't look at her even once and the moment the photograph was clicked, he went away. Resham saw in disgust the way two of her closest friends were behaving, but didn't know how to deal with it. She whispered something in Aarti's ears.

After some time, most of the young guests moved to the DJ stage for a dance. Aarti was very enthusiastic and she danced her way to glory. After a little while, she called Monika and she could not refuse. She was dancing after long and as she tapped her foot, she began enjoying it. While she was lost in dancing, Aarti pulled Gurpeet also on to the stage and bringing him near her, said, "*Maasi*, only *mama* can match your steps and I have brought him here. The two of you will make a wonderful pair."

Looking at her Gurpreet said, "I don't think your *maasi* would like to dance with me. I...I am not fit for her," and was about to go away, when Aarti stopped him, "You have become very silly since a few days, *mama*! I won't talk to both of you if you don't dance with me."

Unable to refuse her, they both danced. Initially, both of them didn't wish to. However, once they began dancing, Monika felt that she was enjoying it – his touch, his fragrance, and his presence...just everything about him. The song ended at that moment. Aarti's friends from school had come over and she was busy with them. He left her standing there and moved away swiftly before she could say anything.

During the *pheras*, they were both placed next to each other once again. However, he did not look at her even once. Monika was going through an inrush of emotions. His presence was making her weak and she hated feebleness in herself. She made herself emotionally strong once again and said to herself, 'This time, I am not going to listen to my heart. My heart is very vulnerable. I will only listen to my mind which commands me not to believe in anyone anymore.'

And then it was *vidai* time. Hugging her tight, Resham cried a lot and said, "Monika, please reconsider your decision. If not for anyone, then for my sake. I will be happy to know that you are happily settled."

She replied, "I know your anxiety for me, dear, but my decision is firm and final. I shall be returning tomorrow with a lot of happy memories. I am so happy that you chose a person like Shantanu as your husband. I am sure that you will be live happily ever after."

After the marriage ceremonies were over, she was extremely tired and slept like a log. She had a flight from Chandigarh in the afternoon and she had to leave in the morning. When she got up, she had not set her luggage and quickly began to arrange it. She wished to take a last look at her bungalow. Shekhar accompanied her. She was mostly quiet during the visit.

After returning, she gave a call to Resham to bid her adieu. Resham's mother did the customary *tika* and gifted her lot of special gifts. With a bagful of memories, Monika sat in the car which was to leave her to Chandigarh for her flight back to Paris. Shekhar was accompanying her.

Did she want to go? The combat between her mind and heart still continued. Whenever Gurpreet's memories came in front of her eyes, it seemed that the heart would win. However, the mind would remind her of the frauds in her life and tossed the heart on the floor. Finally, her mind won. They reached Chandigarh airport by then. Shekhar took her luggage and got a trolley for her. He wheeled her trolley till the entry. She waved at him and said, "See you soon in Paris!"

Shekhar asked, "Monika, are you sure you wish to go to Paris?"

She stated with finality in her tone, "Yes, I do! I mean what you wish for, but no...it isn't going to be..."

□

Epilogue

Monika raised her hand for putting the *jaimala* on Gurpreet's neck, but his friends took him in his lap and raising him high, said, "*Parjai*, it is not so easy to hook our friend! You need to grow taller!"

Monika was perplexed. However Gurpreet shouted, "What kind of friends you are? For Monika, I am even ready to crawl on my knees!"

His friends stated with laughter, "But we are not going to release you!" There was a tussle and Gurpreet managed to free himself from their clutches and bending on his knees, said, "Monika, here I am for you."

Monika blushed and placed the garland around his neck. Gurpreet got up and placed his garland around Monika's neck. They both looked at each other. It was a moment of ultimate happiness and everyone clapped at the holy union.

Aarti invited them both for a dance soon after. This time, both of them got down and danced without any reluctance. Aarti asked, "*Mama*, are you happier this time since *maasi* returned all the way from Delhi?"

Looking into Monika's eyes, Gurpreet replied, "Yes, I undeniably am! Your *maasi* is funny indeed! She refused to listen to everyone and went up to Delhi, only to return back by the next flight. But I am really happy to marry my sweetheart of so many years. And now, please call her as *mami* and not *maasi*."

Monika said, "No, she will call me *maasi* and you are her *maasaji*."

Gurpreet smiled and said, "Whatever makes you happy, dear!"

□□□